I0518207

On Broken Glass

A REIMAGINING OF CINDERELLA

ONCE UPON A FAIRYTALE

SERENE HEINER

CARPE VITAM
PRESS LLC

Copyright © 2024 by Carpe Vitam Press LLC

All rights reserved.

No part of this book may be reproduced in any form or by any electronic or mechanical means, including information storage and retrieval systems, without written permission from the author, except for the use of brief quotations in a book review.

Cover art by: rntyass, Glitter_Klo, Pixa Bay

One

B lake sank into a low squat, attempting to place the stupidly heavy nightstand gently onto the piece of scrap carpet she had brought.

"Come on, Blakely," she panted to herself. "From the legs. Use the legs."

Just as the corner of the dark wood touched the ground, there was the telltale sound of tearing denim.

The rest of the furniture landed with a plop and she straightened, running a hand along the backside of her jeans.

She groaned, feeling where the material had split next to the butt seam.

"Great," she said, wiping sweat-soaked flyaways from her face. "Just great." She tugged on the cropped hem of her t-shirt in a ridiculously idiotic attempt to cover the hole, but the material *obviously* didn't even come close to reaching it.

Blake released the material, which sprang back into place. She tipped her head back, sighing. "Of course you would choose the Wonder Woman underwear today."

Sucking in a deep breath, Blake leaned down and pushed the nightstand toward the elevator, sliding it, shag down, across the tile floor.

The bright side was this apartment complex had an elevator. She'd have to mention the sheer glory of it when she texted the owner, Mamie, and thanked her *again* for letting her have the next available space.

She didn't even care if that made her a charity case. It had an elevator!

Blake pushed the up button then looked down at the nightstand. There was no way she'd be able to push the piece of carpet over the elevator lip. She'd have to pull it in.

She plucked at her filthy t-shirt while she waited. Through the front window of the building, she could see a man approaching the front entrance.

"Crap," she muttered, turning to put her back to the metal doors. Just what she needed. A new neighbor witnessing her finagling a nightstand into an elevator while flashing a peek of bright blue Wonder Woman undies.

The elevator dinged. Still watching the approaching man, she bent over, grabbed the corners of the carpet piece, and with a loud grunt, scooted back into the elevator, butt first, pulling the nightstand in with her.

"Oof," someone grunted.

Blake froze, her backside pushed up against something most definitely *not* a wall.

"For the record," came a deep voice. A *man's* voice. "Most people just shake hands."

Blake snapped up straight, spinning around, her hands instinctively covering the rip in her jeans. "Oh my gosh, I'm so sorry. So, so sorry. I didn't see you there. I was... in a hurry," she finished lamely as the man's lopsided grin grew.

Smile lines appeared by his brown eyes as his tanned skin crinkled. Brown hair flopped over his forehead in messy waves. They lay in such a way that she couldn't tell if it was on purpose or not. Blake blinked, looking away. What was it about good-looking guys that made her try extra hard not to stare? She had this weird theory that handsome men were used to being fawned over and she didn't want to add to their ego.

The elevator tried to close, but the door hit the side of the nightstand.

"Can I help?" the man asked.

Making sure her butt pointed to the empty side of the elevator, Blake bent down and pulled the nightstand all the way inside.

"It's okay," she said, straightening. "I'm just gonna drag it to my apartment. Shouldn't be too hard."

Blake expected the man to excuse himself but he didn't, and the door closed, sealing them both inside. She swallowed, finally allowing herself to really look at him. It would be foolish not to inspect a stranger, especially since she was alone with him.

A dark green t-shirt stretched across his wide chest and thick arms, a large gym bag slung over one shoulder.

"Or you could let me help you," he said, bringing her eyes back to his. They still held a sparkle of mirth, no doubt at her expense. "That way, no other unsuspecting men will get assaulted."

Her mouth popped open, but his smile lines only deepened. Blake narrowed her eyes. "But then you would know where I live. Maybe you're a stalker." She leaned forward. "Or a serial killer who collects pinky toes."

The man's eyes shifted, looking around as though afraid someone would hear them. "Oh, you're good," he whispered. "How did you know?"

There was a teasing light there that made Blake's shoulders relax. She sniffed. "It's my superpower." Might as well run with her underwear theme.

The man's mouth twitched. "Well, your superpower was only slightly off. I deal solely in the black market for used nightstands, not toes." He tapped the piece of furniture between them. "I had my eye on this sexy beast from the moment I... okay, *almost* from the moment I laid eyes on it. I might have been a little distracted at first."

This time, his smile was wide and Blake felt heat stain her cheeks.

"I really am sorry about—"

The doors to the elevator slid open, startling her.

Oh, right. She hadn't actually pushed her floor button. They were still on the main floor and the man she'd initially seen walking toward the building now stood there, staring at them and the block of wood at their feet.

"Uh, hey Cam," the new arrival said, clearly deciding whether he could push his way onto the elevator with his small toolbox. He wore gray cargo pants that were too long for him and a tight blue button-down shirt.

"Hey Wyatt," Cam said, dropping his gym bag and moving the nightstand to make room.

Blake scowled. He could have at least pretended it was a little heavy. She backed up as Cam and her nightstand crowded her into the corner. He smelled nice, like men's deodorant, dryer sheets, and possibility. She crossed her arms. Her thoughts sounded like a freakin' romance novel.

Wyatt nodded his thanks as he moved inside, and Blake read the patch on the arm of his shirt. The Grand Duke's Repair Service. He was tall and thin, with thinning, black hair and a black mustache. He turned and pushed the fourth floor button.

"Mr. King's apartment again?" Cam asked.

Wyatt sighed. "Yup. Seems like he's always breaking something."

His attention shifted to Blake and she couldn't help but run her hands down the backside of her jeans. From the corner of her eye, she saw Cam hide a grin.

"Hi, I'm Wyatt." He extended a hand. Blake wiped her sweaty palm on her pants before accepting, but quickly drew her hand back.

"Blake," she said.

He smiled. "Nice to meet you." Wyatt glanced at the nightstand. "Moving in?"

She nodded. "Yeah." The conversation died, and she swallowed. Wow, wasn't she a super new neighbor. The small talk was just rolling off her in waves. She wanted to roll her eyes at herself.

"Which apartment?" Wyatt asked. "I didn't know there was an opening on the fourth floor."

"Oh," Blake said, realizing she hadn't asked him to push the button to her floor.

"She thinks I'm a serial killer," Cam said.

Wyatt blinked at him. "What?"

"What?" Blake echoed.

Cam shrugged. "I offered to help her bring her furniture to her apartment, but she thinks I'm a serial killer, so she won't tell me where she lives."

Blake almost gaped. "I never said that."

Wyatt's mouth formed a silent "O" as he glanced at the elevator buttons.

Blake crossed her arms, glaring at Cam. "Wyatt, would you mind pushing three for me?"

"Of course," he said, lighting up the third floor button.

Just then, the doors opened to the fourth floor. Wyatt stepped out and turned back, grinning. "Enjoy being neighbors. Oh," he paused, looking at Blake, but pointed at Cam. "He's not a serial killer..." His smile faded. "I don't think—" The elevator doors closed, cutting him off.

Cam threw his head back and laughed. Not just a chuckle, but an honest-to-goodness, full-bellied laugh. Tears gathered in the corner of his eyes while Blake glared at him.

"I'm sorry," Cam said, wiping his eyes. "It's just that Wyatt's going to be wondering about you for weeks."

Blake felt a smile tug at her lips. She didn't want to smile; she wanted to be annoyed, but Cam's laugh loosened something in her chest. Something that had been tightly wound for the last year.

He flustered her, and it was stupid. She didn't even know this guy.

The elevator dinged, opening to the third floor.

"What did he mean when he said to enjoy being neighbors?" Blake asked as she maneuvered around the nightstand, preparing to drag it out of the elevator while keeping her underwear from burning out Cam's eyeballs.

He chuckled again, slung his gym bag back over his shoulder, then picked up the block of furniture as she tugged at the carpet piece. He was *still* smiling as he moved confidently down the hall.

"Hey," she called, hurrying to catch up. "Do you even know where you're go—"

She cut off when he stopped in front of her new apartment and leaned against the doorframe, waiting.

Blake inwardly groaned. "You live on this floor, don't you?"

His smile widened.

Crap. Crapitycrapcrap. "Let me guess," she said, trying to look unaffected. "Next door?"

"Actually, no."

He straightened as she looked at him, feeling both relieved and weirdly disappointed.

"But on this floor, this was the only vacant apartment." He nodded at her door.

"Right," she said, turning the knob and pushing it open for him. She followed Cam inside and hurried around him as his eyes roved over the small stack of boxes she'd already hauled inside.

"Sorry about the mess," she said while pushing aside boxes and bags that had been unceremoniously dropped wherever.

Cam shook his head, setting the nightstand down against the wall. "It's no problem. Moving is supposed to be chaotic, but..." He waved a hand. "Where's all your help?"

Blake cleared her throat and shoved her hands into her back pockets, keeping her butt turned away from Cam.

Ugh. Personal questions.

"It's just me," she admitted. "But it's totally fine. There's not much left to move."

Cam raised his eyebrows, looking around the furniture-less space. "Really? So you've already moved in beds, tables, chairs... couches?"

"Blake?"

They both turned when Ella strode into the living room. The fifteen-year-old had her headphones on, one side removed from her ear, a cell phone in hand. She stopped when she saw Cam.

The look of surprise melted into one of disgusted boredom. "Dad's only been dead a year and you're already bringing men around?"

A sharp pang shot through Blake's chest even as her cheeks heated, but she shot Ella a glare. This was Ella's new defense mechanism: joking about her father's passing, pretending she hadn't been shattered by it.

"Ella, this is Cam. He's... our new neighbor. On this floor," she finished, suddenly feeling incredibly embarrassed by, well, literally everything. Everything from Wonder Woman saying hi from the rip in her jeans, to the fact that she didn't actually have anyone helping her move in, to Ella's snide remarks.

"Wow, Blake. Just, wow," Ella said, looking completely disgusted.

Ignoring the teenager's attitude, Blake said, "Cam, this is Ella. My, um, daughter."

"*Step*-daughter," Ella corrected, looking at her phone to write a text.

The way she emphasized the correction sent a stab of hurt through Blake's chest. Had it really been less than a year ago that Ella had been excited Blake was her mom?

They didn't exactly look alike. Ella was all blonde hair and blue eyes, while Blake had reddish-brown hair and bright green eyes. Plus, Blake was only thirty-one. They kind of looked more like sisters.

"Nice to meet you, Ella," Cam said, holding out his hand to shake hers.

5

Ella didn't even look up from her phone. "Sure. Hey, Blake, Brook is coming to pick me up. We're going to a movie. I'll be back late."

Blake had to force her breathing to stay even. She wished this was a private conversation instead of happening in front of some guy she flashed on an elevator.

"The deal was," she said calmly to Ella, "I would bring up all the boxes and you would put everything away. We need to get it done today and tomorrow. I have work Monday and you start school."

Ella rolled her eyes. "This is stupid. If Tamera was still with us—"

"We've talked about that a hundred times," Blake cut in, praying this conversation wouldn't turn into a fight in front of Cam. "I need your help, Ella."

"Well, Brook is already here," Ella said, throwing up her hands. "And she drove all the way from Cape City. I'm not sending her away." She grabbed her bag off the counter. "I'll be back at eleven."

Blake rubbed her temple. She couldn't do this right now. If she forced Ella to stay, she'd probably put everything away in the wrong places just to make things harder.

"Nine."

Ella made a disgusted sound. "It's not even a school night."

Blake crossed her arms, trying to look intimidating.

"Fine," Ella rolled her eyes. "Ten."

"Nine, or you lose that phone for the rest of the week."

"Ugh!" Ella stormed past her and Cam. As she yanked open the door, she yelled, "You ruin everything!" The door slammed behind her.

Two

S ilence bounced off the walls of the hollow apartment as Blake stared at the door Ella just slammed, willing herself not to scream to ease the pressure squeezing her chest.

Cam stood beside her, quiet and still. Why wouldn't he leave? Now, not only had he seen her superhero underwear, and witnessed her flail at small talk, now he would know what a terrible mom—*step*mom—she was.

At least she wouldn't have to worry about him coming over to borrow things.

"Well," Cam said, and she braced for whatever excuse he would make to get the heck out of this crazy lady's apartment. Or worse... he was going to ask her if she was okay. Then she would have to lie.

"Where might I find the rest of your furniture?"

She blinked, finally looking at him. He appeared perfectly at ease, not a trace of judgment in his eyes. That, more than anything that had happened the last few months, made her want to cry.

Blake cleared her throat. "I got it, really. I'm sure you're late for wherever it was you were going before I—you know." She made a fist, awkwardly bouncing it forward until it slammed into her the open palm of her other hand. "With my... backside."

Cam's eyes did that crinkly thing again as he laughed. "Blake," he said, still chuckling. "Where. Is. Your. Stuff?"

He said each word like it was its own sentence, as if that would somehow make her not argue with him.

She sighed. It was so stupid that it worked. "It's in the moving truck downstairs."

"All of it?" he asked, looking at her like she was going to pull a fast one on him or something.

Blake snorted. She couldn't help it. All of her *stuff* was indeed in the small moving truck outside. It was hard to believe that only a year ago she was living in a giant house with more *stuff* than he could imagine.

"It's important that you're honest with me," Cam said, suddenly looking quite serious. For some reason, it made her heart quicken. Did he know who she was? Only a few local news stations had run stories on her husband's passing.

Cam shook his head. "We serial killers need to know as much about our victims as possible, but I can't have too many people know what I look like. So, if we have to travel somewhere to get the rest of your things, I need to know if I should pack a ski mask or something."

There was a moment of perfect stillness before a laugh burst from Blake. It felt almost foreign, like it was dusty and rusted from unuse. Who was this guy?

"No ski mask needed today," she said, turning to head back to the truck, but as she pulled open the door, Cam said her name.

She turned.

He still stood there, all handsome and smiley. Scratching his head, he chuckled and then pointed to her backside. "For the record, I'm perfectly fine with your current attire. However, if you'd prefer to change into something less... heroic, I'll wait."

Blake drew in a deep breath, shut the door, and without a word, walked around him to find another pair of pants.

* * *

Two hours later, Blake pushed aside a box so Cam and his friend, Ridge, could set down her small couch. Apparently, Ridge had called Cam to meet him at his boxing gym, which was where Cam had been going when she literally bumped into him.

As soon as Cam called back to explain why he wouldn't make it, Ridge had come right over to help. She was still in awe that these men had taken time out of their Saturday to help her. They didn't even know her. She couldn't imagine having a friend she could call like that and they would just drop everything to help.

Her mind drifted to Mamie. Maybe.

All three of them were sweaty and drained, and Blake was already scrambling to think of a way to repay them. She had little money ever since she found out her husband had lost all of his assets just before he died.

"How about I order some pizza?" she asked, as the guys threw the cushions back onto the couch. "To thank you. I mean, I know it's not much, and I... I can pay you. Next week, if you don't mind waiting that long—"

The doorbell rang, cutting off Blake's awkward torrent of words. Cam strode past her and answered it.

Pulling out his wallet, he handed some bills to the gangly pizza guy who passed him three oversized pizza boxes. The delivery guy quickly counted the cash and stammered a thank you for the generous tip.

She just... stared at Cam as he closed the door, her mouth slightly gaped. "When did you—"

He winked. "Serial killers don't reveal their secrets."

Blake puffed out a laugh. "Well, here, I can pay you back—"

"My treat," he said, setting down the steaming boxes. "It's my housewarming gift." He paused, suddenly looking a little sheepish. "If that's alright. I promise I'm not trying to step on your toes."

Ridge walked over and whispered conspiratorially, "Just let him pay. He probably got ones with mushrooms, so it will serve him right." He made a grossed-out face.

Cam shook his head. "What's wrong with you? Mushrooms are the best! They make everything taste better."

Ridge wrinkled his nose. "Okay, Blake. Break the tie for us. Shrooms or no shrooms?"

Both men watched her, and she had the most ridiculous urge to cry again. What the crap was wrong with her? Why did she want their kindness to be genuine so badly? They were strangers. She didn't know them and they didn't know her, but if there was one thing Blake knew about people, it was that no one did anything for free. Everyone expected or wanted something in return.

Still, in this moment, she didn't want to think about that, didn't want to care about that. These two men had helped her and she would do her best to pay them back on her terms before they could request something of her she couldn't pay.

Blake shrugged her shoulders. "First of all, 'shrooms' makes this a very different kind of pizza, but... sorry, Cam. I'm with Ridge on this one. Mushrooms are disgusting."

Ridge gave a whoop of victory while Cam groaned. "Whatever. You guys are missing out." He opened a box, revealing a pizza that looked like it had literally everything on it... including mushrooms.

"You have to at least try a bite," Cam said, waving her over.

Blake made a face as she leaned over the pizza. "I won't like it," she insisted.

"One. Bite."

Again, he said each word like it was its own sentence and, like before, she complied. Grimacing, she bit into the pizza. Almost immediately, she tasted the mushroom, her face screwing up in disgust.

Ridge laughed while Cam looked affronted.

"Sorry," she choked. "It's still not good."

Cam grabbed the box off the top. "More for me."

Ridge opened the next box, then glared up at Cam. "What is this?"

Blake looked inside at the Hawaiian pizza. "Oooh! I love pineapple on my pizza!"

Both of Ridge's hands came up, held stiff as he touched his temples, then chopped the air. "Fruit does not belong on pizza."

"Pineapple does," Blake and Cam said together. Blake laughed as Cam reached over for a high five.

Ridge wrinkled his nose. "You two are not allowed to pick out the pizza next time."

Blake paused. Next time? She grabbed the box before she spent too much time thinking about the words. "More for me," she said, echoing Cam's earlier words.

"There better be something decent in this last box or so help me," Ridge said, opening the lid cautiously, like a monster might leap out of it.

Relief washed over his features. "Finally! Meat lovers!"

Blake dug through the mismatched cardboard boxes scattered throughout the small living room looking for her cups while Cam and Ridge chatted about Ridge's wife and his ideas for a nursery. They were expecting their first baby. As they discussed which tools were going to be needed for the various projects, Blake couldn't help but smile at how excited these grown men were about changing tables and bookshelves. Nothing like her life before or after meeting her late husband. She liked it but she didn't like that she liked it. It was dangerous to want things you could never have.

Ridge's phone dinged. "I better jet," he said after glancing at it. "I promised Isobelle I would help her with a new shipment of books at her bookstore." He stood and Blake did, too.

"Thank you again," she said, extending her hand. "I'll pay y—"

"No need, Blake. I was happy to do it," he said. When Blake opened her mouth to protest, he cut her off. "You don't owe me anything. It's what friends do for each other."

Blake stared at his back as he closed the apartment door behind him. Friends?

An unfamiliar warmth crept into her chest, filling the dark, cold places that had only deepened after Warren's death.

When she turned back around, Cam was placing the used cups into the dishwasher.

"Does Ella like mushrooms?" he asked, walking over to stack the boxes. "If she does, I'll leave this pizza too, but if she doesn't, I'll take it with me. Can't let a masterpiece like this go to waste."

Blake smiled. "I don't think she would eat it. Besides, you paid for them, so they're your pizzas. You should take them all home."

Cam made an exaggerated hurt expression. "Are you rejecting my house-warming gift?" His mouth pulled into a pout. "That cuts deep, Blake."

She laughed and threw up her hands. "Okay, okay, you win. I'll keep the pizzas. Just not the one with the fungus on it."

"Man, why do none of my friends have good taste?" Cam muttered.

Blake's smile faded. There was that word again. Friend. She had the strangest urge to ask him how they could possibly be friends after only knowing each other for a couple of hours, but she held in her words. He would probably think her a total looney.

When Cam turned to look at her, she forced her smile back into place. "Have you ever considered that, being outnumbered as you are, you're the one with the bad taste?"

He screwed his expression into one of deep thought, then shook his head and said, "Nope. It's definitely you guys."

Blake laughed again. When was the last time she'd laughed this much? "I can't thank you enough, Cam. Seriously. I—I truly don't know what to say."

He waved her off. "It was no trouble. Do you need help with anything else? Moving anything around? Returning the truck?"

She shook her head. "I left my car at the rental place and I think you've already put all the heavy stuff where it's gonna stay." She thought of her room and tilted her head from side to side. "Probably. Mostly."

Cam chuckled. "I'm sure you're more than capable of moving your own stuff around, but not only am I a serial killer, I am also a member of the 'Save the Jeans' society, where we strive to save jeans from being overused and overworked, which leads to disparaging rippage."

Blake had to smother her laugh. This man was utterly ridiculous.

"Therefore," Cam continued, unaffected by her snorts, "I am duty bound to request that you text me anytime you need any heavy lifting done." He gave her a stern look. "It's for the safety of the jeans."

Finally laughing outright, Blake just shook her head. "Text you? But I—"

He sighed. "Alright, fine, you can have my number. Geez, you're so pushy. Let's see your phone."

Feeling weirdly speechless and unable to think of a clever comeback, Blake unlocked her phone and handed it to him. He typed on her screen, then pulled his own phone out of his pocket as it buzzed. He unlocked it and typed something. A moment later, her phone buzzed, too. He typed on it again, and his phone buzzed.

She folded her arms and cleared her throat. "Do you always have conversations with yourself?"

Glancing up, he just grinned at her. He sent one more text, then handed her phone back.

"Well, I'll let you get settled in," he said, moving to the door.

Blake ignored the annoying pang in her chest that he was leaving. For a couple of hours, she hadn't felt alone. He opened the door. "Thanks for letting me help."

She just shook her head. Seriously? He gave up his whole Saturday to help her. "Thank *you* for helping and for dinner."

He stepped out while she stayed in the doorway, curious which apartment was his. Cam removed a key from his pocket, stepped across the hall, and slid it into the door across from hers.

Her mouth popped open. Holy. Crap.

He looked back over his shoulder and winked as he opened his own apartment door.

She glared at him as he laughed, mimicking her by leaning on the doorframe.

"I thought you didn't live next door?" Blake accused.

Cam just shrugged. "I don't. I live across the hall."

"I guess this means there's no avoiding you, is there?" She meant to sound teasing, but something dark passed over Cam's expression.

He straightened and shoved the hand not holding the pizza box into his jean pocket. "Look, Blake, if I made you feel uncomfortable in any way—"

"No," she cut in, louder than she'd meant. "It wasn't you, I just meant, you know, after I, well..." She made a fist, bouncing it forward until it hit the open palm of her other hand, just like she'd done before. "With my backside," she finished lamely.

The shadow lifted from Cam's face. "Please don't worry about that. It was one of the nicest hellos I've ever received."

At this, Blake rolled her eyes, but laughed. "I guess I'll see you around, then."

Cam nodded. "I hope so."

Blake closed the door and went back into the kitchen. She picked up her phone and unlocked it to see the text messages Cam had sent.

Blake: Hey Cam, it's Blake. Your new neighbor across the hall. I promise to text you if ever I need help with anything.

Cam: Oh hey, Blake! Yes, I remember you! What a surprise! I will hold you to that promise.

Blake: Well, that's good. Cause I'm stubborn, so this might be a hard promise to keep.

Cam: I have faith in you.

Laughing to herself, Blake started unpacking the kitchen and tried not to think about how, for the first time in far too long, she might have found a friend, and how much it was going to hurt when he left.

Because they always did.

Three

"Ella!" Blake called while rummaging through the piles of papers and kitchen items still waiting to be organized into cupboards and drawers littering the counter. Dang it! She just had the keys in her hand. "Ugh, I always do this," she muttered.

She spun to find Ella storming into the living room. "I can't go to school like this."

Blake scrunched her brows together. "Like what? You look cute. Those are the clothes you just picked out."

"Yeah," Ella said. "From the *thrift store*."

Blake sighed. Not this again. Ella had gone through a growth spurt a couple months ago and they hadn't had the money to do the kind of shopping she was used to. "You liked them when we picked them out. Besides, you can't even tell they're not brand new."

Ella flipped her blonde hair out of her face. "Brook said people can always tell. What if everyone at the new school knows we're poor now?"

Lifting the apartment agreement papers, Blake spotted her keys. "No one will be able to tell they came from a thrift store."

"I still don't see why I have to change schools. There's only a couple months left in the school year! I could have stayed where I was."

Blake faced her, fighting to keep her voice even. "You already know why that wouldn't work. I can't drive you all the way over there and make it to my job on time."

Ella snatched up her backpack. "Fine." As she moved past Blake, she muttered, "Try not to sell off the rest of my belongings while I'm gone."

A defense formed on Blake's tongue even as the apartment door slammed shut, but she swallowed it down. Ella needed someone to be mad at. Her dad's bad choices had turned her whole life upside down, but she didn't need to know that. Not yet. She was still grieving. No, Blake could be the "horrible stepmother" for a while longer.

The drive to Ella's new school was quiet, except for Ella's angry tapping on her phone. She made Blake stop the car around the corner from the school, embarrassed to be seen in their used Toyota Camry. Blake's grip tightened on the steering wheel, but she clenched her teeth and said nothing as minivans and rusty trucks pulled through the dropoff and parked in the lot. This was a public school, not the hoity-toity private schools Ella had grown up in. Still, she said nothing, just pulled over against the curb.

Her stepdaughter said nothing as she climbed out and walked away.

"Ella," Blake called, knowing she could still hear her. "Shut your door!" But the girl just kept walking.

Grinding her teeth, Blake unbuckled her seatbelt and jumped out to shut the passenger door.

Pulling away from the school, she blew out a sharp breath. There wasn't time to stew over Ella's attitude. She was already running late. She put the first address on her list into her GPS and turned the car towards the other end of the city.

The driveway she pulled into was long with a grand house perched on the side of the hill, flaunting its pillars and great arches like a peacock would its feathers.

Not long ago, she lived in a house much like this one. It hadn't been quite so large or quite so grand, and Blake had liked that about it. Warren had had money, but even he had been a smaller fish in the upper class pool.

Drawing in a deep breath, Blake parked, per instructions, by the garage door. She grabbed the cleaning supplies from the back of her car and headed toward the side door.

She held back a snort that it had its own doorbell.

After a moment, a woman came to the door. Her face pinched, like she was sucking on a lemon for the fun of it.

Blake smiled and said hello, even as the woman's eye's traveled over her, as though checking to see if her black shirt, black pants, or black shoes carried anything as offensive as a piece of lint.

"I'm Blake, from the Invisible Maid Service," Blake said, forcing a smile.

"You're late," was all the woman said, and moved aside.

Inhaling slowly, Blake stepped through the door, reminding herself she'd had way, way worse jobs than this.

Several hours later, she pulled into her second driveway of the day. They'd changed her route, sending her a new address at the last minute.

Stuffing the last of her homemade peanut butter sandwich into her mouth, she brushed the crumbs from her pants as she parked.

Cleaning mansions was tedious, but it paid well. Even though Blake wasn't one for calling in favors and asking for help, she had asked the maid who'd always cleaned Warren's house who she worked for and if they were hiring.

Blake was wiping down a shiny black grand piano when she heard her name. She froze, her rag leaving a streak of wax.

"Blake? Is that you?"

Slowly, she turned around, braced to face whoever was there.

She blew out a sharp breath. "Mamie?"

The woman before her was in her early 70s and had more energy than most people Blake knew who were half the woman's age.

"Blake! It is you!" Mamie came straight for her, *very* high heels clicking on the tile floor. Without preamble, she pulled Blake into a massive hug, holding her so tight it was actually a bit hard to breathe.

Blake didn't bother pulling away. Mamie would let go when she was ready. That's just how she was. Mamie was the perfect mix of class and snark. The woman was an army vet who started making money selling Mary Kay but then moved into real estate. Her husband was a grumpy ole' badger, but his investments definitely paid off nicely. At least, that's what Mamie said.

She'd met this woman after Warren's death. Blake had been sitting in the corner of a coffee shop, fighting back tears as she'd tried to figure out how to tell Ella they'd need to sell the home she'd grown up in. She just couldn't afford the bills and the taxes.

Mamie had plunked herself in the seat across from her and asked her if she was okay.

At first, Blake tried to assure this stranger that she was fine, but then she blinked and somehow, Mamie had produced Blake's favorite pastry. Not wanting to be rude, she took a small bite and after that, Blake's entire life story had spilled out, including how she needed to find an affordable apartment.

Mamie promised to let her know as soon as there was an opening at any of her complexes.

The day after the house sold, Mamie called to say there would be a vacancy on the same date they needed to be out of the house. It had all seemed too fantastical, too good to be true. And yet, here they were.

Finally, Mamie released her. "Oh, it's so good to see you!"

"It's good to see you too," Blake said, feeling overwhelmed by this woman's generosity.

Mamie grinned. "How are you settling into the new apartment? Is there anything wrong with it? Do you still need help moving in? I know you wouldn't let me hire anyone to help you, but you know I would in a second."

Blake shook her head. "I know, but we're good. A neighbor helped me out."

Mamie's eyes sparkled. "New neighbor, huh? Is he cute?" She gripped Blake's arm. "Did he ask you out?"

"Mamie!" Blake laughed.

The older woman scowled playfully. "What? I have to live vicariously through you, young lady. My husband is all vinegar these days. Never wants to do anything." Her large, glittery earring winked as she talked. "So, tell me all about him."

Blake arched an eyebrow. "Who said the neighbor who helped me was a him?"

Mamie's smile faded. "Wait, it wasn't?" She looked away, muttering. "Well," she said with a sigh. "How's Ella?"

Blake's smile faded. "She's... struggling. She really, really doesn't like me right now, but I know it's because she doesn't have all the facts and she's still grieving."

Mamie touched her arm. "When are you going to tell her about the money?"

"I don't know," Blake said, shaking her head. "How do you tell a girl that the man she adored more than anything lost her inheritance in dirty business deals, then gambled away the rest of his money trying to get it back?" She rubbed her eyes. "It's still hard for me to wrap my head around that. Warren didn't seem the gambling type. Even when he told me about the cancer, he said Ella and I were both financially set and we wouldn't have to worry." She sighed. "Maybe everyone is a liar and I just can't ever see it."

Mamie was quiet for a moment. "Whatever happened to those two secretaries of his? The ones you said disappeared after the funeral."

"Anna and Zelle?" Blake shrugged. "I don't know. I haven't seen either of them for a long time." She tilted her head, remembering. "Anna texted me once, not that long ago, asking if she could go through Warren's office at the house, but we had already moved his stuff into storage. "

"Why did she want to do that?" Mamie asked.

Blake shrugged. "Something about some paperwork for her taxes."

"I see," Mamie said, her words slow and thoughtful.

Just thinking about all of that made Blake's shoulders droop. Warren had only been gone a short while when lawyers and bankers swooped in, demanding information about the company and money, and Blake couldn't help them at all. Even though the company had to declare bankruptcy, Blake was left with a mountain of gambling debt.

She looked at her feet. "I don't know what to do. Ella was already grieving and angry at me for not telling her about the cancer, so when she saw me selling stuff, she decided I was the villain." She shrugged. "Maybe I am."

"Oh, stop that," Mamie chided. "You are not." She gripped her shoulders. "You're a woman who's been dealt a rough hand in life and doing the best you can with it all."

Blake nodded, still wondering why she had told this woman so much about herself that day in the coffee shop. Especially about her family. She rarely told people about them. Nobody likes to talk about parents who treated their kid like a burden instead of a blessing.

"Yeah," was all she said because, in truth, all she could see were the ways she was failing at everything, especially with Ella.

Mamie's eyes narrowed. "And money? Are you..."

"We're making it work," Blake assured her. It wasn't entirely true and the other woman's expression said she could see through the lie. Still, Mamie was gracious and just said, "Well, that's good."

That night, long after Ella had gone to sleep, Blake sat on her bed, piles of bills spread out before her. She never liked math, but since when did life ever care about what she liked or what she wanted?

If she was careful, they might be able to pay all their bills this month, but there wouldn't be anything left to throw at the debt pile. Unless she got rid of the storage unit. That meant she would need to go through all of Warren's things, which she really didn't want to do. She needed to find a second job, or at least one that paid more.

Most of Warren's life insurance money had gone towards paying for the funeral. And medical bills. And doctor's bills, both holistic and medicinal. And medications and special treatments. And the extravagant, last-minute trips they'd taken to spend time together that had been charged to a credit card Blake had no way of paying off.

She also set aside a small portion of it for Ella to have when she turned eighteen. Once that was done, there was nothing left.

She rubbed her burning eyes. If it was just her, she could do it, but she had Ella. She had to take care of someone else besides herself and that, more than anything, felt the heaviest. How was she supposed to do this? She knew nothing about raising a kid—a teenager! Let alone one that hated her.

Blake laid down and curled into a ball, ignoring the papers still scattered around her. In the morning, she would be strong, but here, alone in the dark, she allowed herself to crumble.

Four

A week later, Blake pushed open the apartment door and was greeted by voices. Ella's, at least, she recognized.

She turned the corner to find her stepdaughter sitting on the couch while a boy rested his head in her lap. He was holding up a phone so they could both see the screen.

"I love that one," Ella said, blushing when the boy tilted his head to look back and up at her.

"Wait, wait," he said. "This one is better." He tapped his phone screen and music spilled into the room.

They both watched for a moment then he said, "Here it comes..."

Whoever was singing in the video belted out a high note and Ella gasped. "Whoa, that was ah-mazing! You are so good! I can't believe you're not famous yet."

The boy shrugged. "I will be, someday."

Ella looked up and saw Blake standing there. Her face went white and she hurried to stand up, pushing the boy's head off her lap.

For her part, Blake wasn't sure what to think or what to feel. Navigating motherhood was tricky enough, but now there were teen boys too? Her own high school experience had been less than stellar.

Her parent's apathetic approach to parenting had forced her to grow up fast. In high school she naively assumed she understood people in a way most didn't. She'd believed she was smarter than the ones who ended up in terrible relationships, but perhaps that's what all youth thought.

Now, she knew better. Knew that no one gave selflessly, that there was always a catch, especially in relationships. She was someone no one was willing to fight for. Not her parents, not the men she'd dated... except maybe Warren. But even with Warren it felt sometimes like he had been looking for a mother to his child more than a wife for himself.

Still, he'd been good to her, they'd been good together, and she missed the life they'd shared.

"Hey," Blake said, moving aside the cereal box and empty bowls so she could set her bag on the counter. It was clear Ella hadn't done any cleaning since she'd gotten home from school. "Who's this?"

The boy had scrambled to his feet after Ella had all but tossed him off her.

"Blake," Ella stammered. "This is Prince. We met at school."

The boy extended his hand. "Nice to meet you."

Blake shook it. "Prince?"

The boy laughed. He was cute, no question. He had the whole square-jaw-broad-shoulder thing going on, but he also seemed to know it, which automatically made Blake apprehensive.

"It's my band name. I'm the lead singer." He puffed out his chest.

She tried not to groan. Of course he would be in a band. What's more cliche than a high school guy in a garage band?

"Oh," Blake offered, trying to sound... How was she trying to sound?

"Yeah. Maybe you've heard of us," Prince said. "Royal-T. We have a youtube channel."

He was smiling at her like she *should* know his band and that she *would* be awed by his presence.

"That's... impressive," she said, weakly.

Prince nodded, flashing another dimpled smile. "Well, I better go," he said. "It was nice getting to know you better, Ella. I'll see you tomorrow."

Ella blushed all the way to the roots of her blonde hair. "Okay, yeah. See ya. Thanks for the ride home."

When Prince was gone, Blake tried not to roll her eyes just thinking of his name, and turned to Ella. "You ignored all of my calls and texts. You turned off your location. I stopped by the school to pick you up but you weren't there."

Ella huffed. "I texted you that I was getting a ride home instead of taking the bus."

Blake pulled out her phone and opened her messages. "No, you didn't."

"I guess I forgot, chill," Ella said, throwing up her hands.

Blake ground her teeth. "I was trying to help since you told me you hated the bus. If you didn't want me to come, you should have just said so."

"Okay, fine," Ella said, typing on her phone. "I don't want you to come."

Moving closer, Blake pressed her hands together, fighting to remain calm. "I know all of this is hard, and I am glad you made a friend. Just... be careful, especially with boys. You probably shouldn't be alone with him until you get to know him better."

Ella scowled. "I do know him."

"You *just* met him."

"So? Are you saying you can't know someone's heart the moment you meet them?"

It took everything Blake had not to laugh at Ella's naivety. "That's exactly what I'm saying"

Shaking her head, Ella stormed past her. "You're such a hypocrite. That Cam guy was over here the very first day we moved here and you guys were alone."

"He was helping me move furniture, not laying in my lap."

"You don't know anything!" she shouted over her shoulder.

"Don't walk away while we're having a conversation," Blake snapped, making the girl pause, her face murderous. Blake rubbed her temple. "Look, a lot's happened, and I know you miss your dad—"

"Don't tell me what I'm feeling," Ella ground out through clenched teeth, but Blake saw the tears gathering in her eyes, making her heart ache.

Instinctively, she reached for the girl who, only a year ago, would have happily run into her arms. They would have cried together.

But Ella jerked away. "You're not my mom." Her bedroom door slammed shut.

Blake alone stood in the middle of their messy apartment. She should tell Ella she needed to do her chores, to come help with dinner, to do her homework, but she just stood there, feeling the profound loneliness that had been her companion her whole life. Until Warren. Until Ella.

She rubbed the ache in her chest. She'd been so used to it before, but she'd allowed herself to believe she'd found a home, a family. The pain was more potent now that all that was gone. She was alone again, and it hurt so much worse.

She walked to the window, trying not to think at all. She watched the traffic stream by and a woman who sat smoking in her rusted, black car, parked across the street.

Her phone dinged. She pulled it from her pocket with a weary sigh but then her pulse quickened when Cam's name appeared on the screen.

For a moment she resisted opening the message. Ella's accusations of Cam were still sharp in her mind. Why would a guy like this even want to talk to a woman with such a disaster of a life?

Shaking off her stupidity, Blake opened the message.

Cam: Do you know anything about cats?

Out of all of the things she could have imagined him texting her about, this was not it. She chuckled as she texted him back.

Blake: Of course I do. Not only am I Wonder Woman, I also work part time as Catwoman.

As soon as she sent the message, three dots materialized, indicating he was typing his response. She reread his first messages while she waited. They still made her smile.

Cam: Ah, multiple identities. Puuuuuurfect.

"Oh my gosh," she said to herself, shaking her head at his stupid joke. There came a knock on the door and, with effort, Blake reined in her smile as she opened the door.

Cam stood there, hands in his pockets, a lopsided grin on his face. Her heart skipped a beat. Why did guys always look so good in black henleys?

He shook his head. "No black leather? Too bad."

She pursed her lips and held up her phone. "Puuurfect? Really?"

He grinned. "I need some advice on befriending a feline companion. I'm not kitten around—"

"Don't." Blake held up her hand as if she could physically ward off more terrible puns.

"Right meow," he finished.

She laughed. How did he always manage to pull them from her? "Those are the worst puns I've ever heard," she said, shaking her head.

His eyes went wide. "Oh, I have way worse ones if you want to—"

"Nope, I'm good."

The whole conversation was dumb and she loved it so much.

From across the hall, something shattered in Cam's apartment. He groaned. "Yeah, I'm gonna need your Catwoman expertise." He turned and raced through the door he'd left ajar. Blake followed.

A dark gray cat was pressed into the corner of the kitchen windowsill, its ears flattened against its head, a shattered drinking glass on the floor below it.

"You little devil," Cam said, stalking to his pantry and pulling out a broom.

The cat hissed at him while he swept up the mess.

"Don't give me that," Cam said, wagging a finger at the animal. "That's the third one you've broken! I'm not going to have anything left to drink out of if you keep this up," he muttered.

Blake glanced around the apartment. The space was a perfect mirror of her own apartment's layout, but nothing about this space looked anything like hers. The walls had been painted a dark moody blue that matched the rich wood floors. A cream sectional perched on a plush rug had perfectly coordinated leather and woven throw pillows. A massive TV hung on the wall over a low cabinet displaying an impressive collection of books. Just off the living room an ornate table runner ran the length of a wooden dining table. She stopped at that one. Since when did a guy use table runners?

Did he have a girlfriend? Her stomach twisted and she was surprised by how much the thought hurt. What had she just told Ella about getting to know someone?

The cat stopped hissing as soon as Cam put the broom away. "You let Ridge talk you into fostering a cat one time and you end up with this ball of angry fluff and fur. Ridge says Isobelle is looking for a foster home replacement but I guess people aren't too excited about having all of their glassware smashed to pieces." Cam eyed the creature. "It's like he's Lucifer personified."

This made Blake smile, despite the tightness in her chest. "Lucifer? Is that his name, then?"

"It should be," he agreed. "Especially because he doesn't like anyone."

Blake looked at the gray cat, watching them with wide, liquid eyes. She recognized a kindred spirit. She knew what it felt like to be unsure if where you lived was where you belonged. She approached slowly. It got up on all fours, pushing itself further into the corner. It didn't hiss at her, though. Truth be told, she knew nothing about cats other than they always land on their feet but when she held out her hand, the animal lifted its head toward her fingers, sniffing. After a moment, the cat allowed her to pet it. His ears perked back up and he lowered his hind haunches.

She turned to find Cam staring at her, mouth gaping open like a caught fish.

He met her eyes. "Lucifer likes you."

Blake lifted her eyebrows. "You forget that I'm catwoman."

A mischievous grin spread across Cam's face. "I'll believe it when I see the black leather with my own eyes."

Blake eyed the table runner then looked around the apartment again, noticing a family photo on the wall. She walked over to it, Lucifer jumping down to follow her.

It was a family of five, all smiles standing in a field of tall grass and wildflowers. A large red barn stood tall and grand in the distance behind them. She recognized a gapped-tooth, grinning boy with a paisley bowtie to be a younger version of Cam. "Your family?" she asked.

Cam moved up beside her. "Yeah. My folks have a ranch outside of town. My sister's got a place out there too and works on the ranch with my parents. Even with my sister's help, it's more work than they can do. I go back and forth, helping out as much as I can. When my sister comes into town she likes to come by and decorate my place. Apparently a card table and folding chairs aren't considered..." He made air quotation marks with his fingers. "Real furniture."

"Ahhh..." Blake said, the tight coil in her stomach loosening. "That explains the table runner."

Cam glanced behind them at his table, his face scrunching up. "Is that what that thing is called?"

Grinning, Blake turned back to the photo. "Who's this?" She pointed to the third boy in the photo. He looked to be the oldest of the three. Silence greeted her question and she glanced at Cam, who wore an expression she knew well.

She swallowed, knowing what he would say before he said it.

"That's Steven," Cam said. "He passed away six years, three months... five days ago."

His voice had gone so soft, and his eyes so distant, Blake knew that he was lost to memories and was sinking, sinking...

She touched his arm, showing rather than saying how sorry she was. Cam looked at her fingers on his arm and for a moment, she was afraid she'd done the wrong thing. Instead, he drew in a slow breath and set his warm hand on top of hers, gripping it like a lifeline. Finally, he cleared his throat and let go. "What about you, Blake? Any siblings?"

This time it was her turn to tense. Personal questions, no thanks. She was usually quite skilled at avoiding them or changing the conversation, but after hearing about Steven, she felt like she at least owed him the truth.

"No. My parents... never really wanted kids." That was all she offered and it felt like too much. Already his grief had shifted and he turned his attention to her. She didn't want him to ask more questions.

"Wait," she said, cutting off Cam as he opened his mouth to respond. "If you grew up on a ranch, shouldn't you be used to animals? Cats, even?"

"Oh, I love cats," Cam said. "That," he pointed to Lucifer, "is not a cat. It's a demon."

The furry beast hissed at him.

"See?"

Blake laughed, even as he scowled and asked, "Want a pet?"

She backed away from him. "No, no. I can't. I already have one feral creature living in my apartment, I don't need two."

Cam grinned. "Fair enough."

Five

Blake's phone buzzed.

Ella: Going to Prince's house after school to listen to his band. Pick me up at 7.

She snorted. "Well, hello to you too. You're welcome for making you lunch today since you slept in... again," she muttered.

Blake: Are you asking me or telling me?

She refrained from sending an annoyed face emoji.

Ella: Can you, will you, oh great and powerful stepmother, controller of my life, slave driver of chores, be so kind and generous as to deem me worthy enough of your time to pick me up at seven on this night?

Blake: You might want to take a moment to remember who pays the phone bill, and who might stop paying the phone bill.

Ella: Could you please just pick me up at 7?

Blake: Yes. Send me the address.

Blake dropped her phone into the cup holder of her car more forcefully than necessary. She loved that kid, but right now, she just wanted to strangle some sense into her. They'd only been here a few weeks but Prince had already become that girl's whole existence. And she was as moody as ever.

Taking another bite of her peanut butter and jelly sandwich, Blake jerked on her seat belt, but she'd pulled too hard too fast and it locked. Annoyed, she unbuckled it with force, if such a thing is possible.

Her chewing slowed and she forced herself to be calm. She watched the light traffic pass by and the people moving past the shops in the strip mall.

Her phone rang and she jumped. "Holy crap," she muttered, her heart racing.

She snatched it up. "Hello?"

"Hello, this is Sherry from Lock Box Storage Facility. Is this Blakely Johnston?"

Blake blinked. "Um, yes, this is her."

"I'm just calling to let you know that we caught someone on our camera's attempting to get into your storage unit. It doesn't look like they did. We've also investigated it ourselves. It appears that your lock is still in place."

"They?"

"Yes ma'am. There were two perpetrators."

Blake drew her brows together. Why would someone want to break into their storage unit?

"Was it just my unit or did they try to get into others?" Blake asked.

Sherry was quiet for a moment but Blake could hear the woman typing on her keyboard.

"It looks like they stopped at another unit but didn't attempt to break into that one. Anyway, we just want to encourage you to check on your unit to make sure everything's okay and assure you that we are increasing our security to ensure this doesn't happen again."

"Oh, alright. Thank you."

"Of course. Have a good day, ma'am. Bye bye."

"Bye," Blake repeated back, but she felt a little numb. It was probably just chance that hers was one of the units being targeted. Still, she needed to check it out. No, she needed to empty it and take one more bill off her plate.

* * *

Blake pulled up to the address Ella had sent her. It wasn't hard to find as it was the only home in the subdivision with an open garage sporting a boy band.

Ella and a cluster of other teens sat in camp chairs on the driveway, watching with rapt, adoring attention.

"Oh boy," Blake muttered, unstrapping her seatbelt. There were four boys in the band. Prince bellowed into a microphone while a drummer beat madly on a black drum set. Two other boys held electric guitars. Yup, just your average high school boy band.

She walked up behind Ella, and Prince looked up. Without missing a note, he grinned and winked at her. Blake fought to not wrinkle her nose.

He wasn't really a bad singer, but he could benefit from some coaching.

Ella started singing along with Prince, quiet, just to herself. Before Warren had passed, Ella was in private voice lessons. They wouldn't sound half bad together–not that Blake would ever say that. Something about this boy set her on edge.

The song finished and Ella and the others leapt to their feet, clapping and cheering wildly. Grinning, Prince strode out of the garage and threw an arm around Ella, tugging her in close. Blake bristled.

"Good to see you again, Mrs. J." Prince said, nodding at her. Ella barely spared her a glance. She was too busy ogling at Prince.

"So, this is the rest of your band?" Blake asked. If her stepdaughter was going to hang out with these kids, she wanted to know who they were.

"Oh, yeah," Prince said, swinging back to look at them as if he just remembered they existed. "That's Jack." He pointed to one of the guitarists. He was a slim boy with a mass of straight hair that flopped into his eyes. Jack offered a shy smile, his gaze cutting to Ella as he waved at them. The moon-eyed look he gave her stepdaughter wasn't lost on Blake, but Ella didn't notice.

"That's Bruno," Prince continued, pointing to the other kid with a guitar. He was tall and lanky, with long brown hair and large ears that stuck out. He gave her a wide, toothy smile, making her think of an overgrown hound.

"And that," Prince said, aiming his finger at the drummer, "is Gus."

The boy was short and round, and he struggled to remove himself from his seat without knocking something over. When he successfully extracted himself, he jumped over some free weights that had been pushed aside and hurried over and shook her hand enthusiastically.

"It's nice to meet you, Ella's mom!"

"Stepmom," Ella cut in.

"It's a pleasure to meet you all," Blake said, nodding to the boys.

"Thanks for letting Ella come over," Prince said, not bothering to introduce any of the other kids there, then looked at her stepdaughter. "See you Friday night?"

Ella practically turned into a puddle. "Definitely."

"Great," he said, finally removing his arm.

As soon as they got in the car, Ella's dreamy expression vanished and she pulled out her phone, ignoring Blake.

"What's Friday night?" she asked when it was clear no information would be volunteered.

Without looking up from her phone, Ella said, "Royal-T is playing at the talent show at the school."

"Ah."

Silence.

"The other guys in the band seem nice," Blake offered, thinking of the way Jack had looked at Ella.

She shrugged. "Yeah, I guess so."

Blake sighed. It was like pulling teeth. "Did you know any of the other kids there?"

"A few," Ella said, finally looking up to grin at her. "But I'm Prince's favorite."

Blake pursed her lips. "I see. And who was his favorite before you? One of them?"

"Ha!" Ella said, looking up from her phone. "Prince has never shown an ounce of interest in any of them but they follow him around like lovesick puppies."

"Sounds like someone else I know," Blake muttered softly enough Ella didn't hear.

As soon as she put the car into park, before she'd even turned off the engine, Ella climbed out, slamming the door behind her.

Blake blew out a sharp breath and watched her walk away. Would things ever get easier? Probably not for a long while.

A sharp knock on her window made her jump, a small scream escaping.

She turned to find Cam standing outside her car door. He waved as she pressed a hand to her racing heart and rolled down her window. "You scared me!"

He chuckled. "Sorry. I didn't realize I was so stealthy." He studied her face, his smile fading. Whatever he saw there made him ask if he could join her. She nodded. The adrenaline rush must have brought emotions to the surface because nothing felt neatly locked away like it had been.

Cam climbed into the passenger seat, his knees crammed in tight.

She laughed. "You can scoot the seat back."

He did.

There was a moment of awkward silence. "Is this how you take your victims?" she asked. "You climb into their cars and then..." She made a stabbing motion in the air.

Cam snorted. "Hardly. I'm far more sophisticated than that."

"Oh really."

"Yes," he insisted, looking miffed. "I usually ask them what's wrong, and then they tell me all about themselves and about all the things weighing them down. I mean, I gotta get their whole backstory first."

Her smile faded. "What if they have nothing interesting to tell? What if they are completely unremarkable?"

He gave her an "oh please" look. "That's simply not true of anybody."

Blake looked down at her hands. Was he honestly trying to be her friend? Was he honestly curious about her and her life? Or did he just... want something.

"Ella seems like a good kid going through hard stuff. How long were you married to her dad?" Cam asked, surprising her. Did he really want to know such things?

"Eight months," she said. "We'd only been married two months when he found out he had pancreatic cancer."

Cam blew out a long breath. "Wow, that's heavy. I'm sorry."

Blake shrugged, playing with her keys. There was an ache in her chest, like a giant bubble of pressure pushed against her ribs. She just wanted some relief; she wanted to tell someone about it. No, not someone. She wanted to tell Cam. She'd only known him a short time but he had never asked anything of her, just... offered to be there if she needed something.

"His name was Warren," she said, slowly, pausing to see if he would cut her off, saying he had somewhere else to be, that he didn't have time like her parents always did when she tried to talk to them. But, he didn't. He sat there, waiting for her to continue.

She cleared her throat. "He asked me not to tell Ella about the cancer. He said he wanted to look into any and all possible treatments first. He didn't want her to worry and said he would tell her when he was ready." She huffed a soft laugh. "He waited a little too long and passed just days after being admitted into the hospital. Ella hardly had a chance to comprehend what was happening before he was gone."

She pushed the keys around with her fingers, surprised by how badly she wanted to cry. She'd learned early in life people didn't like criers. She was always being told to be tough, suck it up, life was hard. But man, just for a moment she wanted to shatter.

"Everything happened so fast," she said, blinking hard. She would not cry, no matter how much she wanted to. "After the funeral, I thought we would have time to grieve, especially Ella. She'd lost both her parents. I mean, mine were dismissive and never around, but they're alive. Ella's father loved her so much. That loss has to hurt so much more."

Cam touched her hand softly. She almost flinched.

"I don't think it's a matter of hurting more," he said. "It's just a different pain. Not being loved hurts. Being loved then losing it hurts."

Well, crap. No one had ever acknowledged the gaping hole in her heart before. A tear slipped down her cheek, splattering onto her pants. Blake didn't move for a long time, fighting to regain control. When she was sure her voice would be steady, she continued, needing to finish the story for some reason.

"Warren was ten years older than me," she said, glancing at Cam again to see his reaction, expecting to find judgment. The age gap wasn't outrageous but it was usually enough to raise eyebrows or earn a scowl.

He just nodded for her to continue. "He was the kindest person I'd ever known. When we met I was working two jobs and going to school." She gave a wry smile. "Yes, I was the waitress being yelled at by some jerk, and he was the nice guy who over tipped because he heard it all. I'd run after him to give him his money back but he insisted I keep it. He and Ella came back often after that. Eventually, he asked me out."

"So, like a romantic comedy or a heartfelt drama," Cam said.

Blake arched her brows.

"What?" he asked with mock offense. "I have a sister. I know what rom coms are."

She laughed. "More heartfelt drama. He wasn't quite romantic himself, and I could tell he liked me, but was cautious. His wife hadn't exactly been a loving person and had walked out on them when Ella was just a baby. When Warren proposed, I thought I'd finally found a family that wanted me. A home." She shrugged and looked at her fingers. "Then he was gone and the only person I have left hates me."

"Sounds like a Charlotte Bronte novel," Cam said, and again, Blake could only stare.

He laughed. "My mom is obsessed with those old classics. She used to make us watch all those regency movies as a family. Still does during the holidays." He leaned close and whispered, "I've seen Pride and Prejudice at least a hundred times."

Blake chuckled at that. "Your mom sounds awesome." Her smile faded. "Warren was kind and steady. Which is why when the lawyers and police came to me to tell me that he had lost his business to some shady deals and had acquired a mountain of gambling debts, I was... shocked. He didn't seem the type, nor had I seen any indication that he was under financial stress." She shrugged. "Maybe I'm just a bad judge of character."

Cam nodded solemnly. "I can see that, Wonder Woman."

Blake reached over to push his shoulder.

He shrugged, his face all innocence. "You invited a serial killer to sit with you in your car."

That pulled another laugh from her. Dang, he was good at that.

"Is that why Ella is so angry?" he asked.

Slowly, Blake shook her head. "No. I haven't told her about the money. At first I thought we could sell the things we could live without. I sold the furniture, all of the home electronics, all of the jewelry and watches. I really thought we could make it but in the end, there was too much debt, too many creditors, and I was forced to sell the house."

She sighed. "The worst part is, a few months after his death she overheard me on the phone with a lawyer when I said I'd known about Warren's cancer almost from the beginning. *That* is why she hates me. I betrayed her trust by not telling her. She blames me for not having been more prepared for it."

"That's not fair," Cam said. "You were just doing what Warren wanted. How were you to know how things would play out?"

"It doesn't matter," Blake replied. "She's hurting and angry, and I'm the only one left to be mad at. She thinks I lost all her father's money. The worst was losing the house and the nanny she'd had since her mother left. I did try to explain once but she's not in a place where she'll listen to anything I say."

"How come Warren's extended family isn't helping?" Cam asked.

She shrugged. "I think he has an aunt who lives in a home, but other than that, I don't think he was in contact with any. I never met any other family members and he didn't bring it up. Our marriage was at the courthouse with a couple of his friends and two of the secretaries from his office. My parents never responded to the invitation."

Cam was silent for a long time and she braced for whatever condemnation was about to come from his mouth.

Blake was surprised when he said, "I'm sorry. That's a lot, and quite frankly, really unfair to you."

Ugh! She was going to cry for real if he didn't stop. For the second time, Cam acknowledged something no one else had.

It cracked her walls.

This time when Cam slid his hand over hers, he kept it there. She looked up, surprised he hadn't run away yet.

"It's okay not to be okay."

His words were so genuine that it broke her. She shook her head as the tears fell. Cam leaned over and pulled her against him, which was awkward sitting in the car as they were, but still, his chest was warm against her cheek, his hand gentle on her back. For the first time in years, she cried.

Six

"**B**lake!"

Blake moved the toothbrush in circles over her teeth as she turned to find Ella skipping her way into the bathroom. A huge smile was spread across her face, reminding Blake of the girl she was before her father passed away.

"You'll never guess what just happened." Her blue eyes were wide with excitement.

Blake spit out the toothpaste. "You actually found a monster under your bed? You always wanted to." She couldn't help but return the smile.

Ella rolled her eyes. "Prince just asked me to junior prom!" She squealed and actually twirled. "I'm only a sophomore and he asked *me*!"

Blake bit down on her toothbrush, hard. "When is prom?" she managed, then rinsed out her mouth.

"Two weeks. Oh my gosh, I'm so excited! Can we go dress shopping? Oh! Nails. I haven't had my nails done in ages!"

The more she prattled on, the more Blake's heart fell. They barely had money for groceries and rent right now. How in the world would she come up with the money for a dress and shoes?

Ella noticed her expression, her own excitement fading. "You're going to tell me we can't afford it, aren't you."

Blake hated the way her smile turned into a glare. Of course it was hard that they didn't have the money, but Ella could at least try to be a little understanding about that.

"I'll... try to pick up a couple extra shifts, then maybe we can go next week and see what's at the thrift store."

Ella huffed. "Forget it. I'll see if one of my mom's old dresses will work."

Warren had kept a couple of his wife's things in case Ella wanted them when she was older.

"I can help you," Blake offered, trying to salvage the moment. "We can find one you like and fix it up—

"I don't need your help," Ella said, turning away.

"Would you stop it?" Blake snapped following her into the living room. She hated how quickly these moments turned. "I'm doing the best I can with everything."

Ella whirled around. "If you hadn't lost all of Dad's money in the first place we wouldn't be living in this dump and Tamera would still be here. Your best is crap!"

That hurt. "Look, I'm sorry about your nanny," Blake shot back. "But I didn't lose the money and this isn't a dump!" Her frustration mounted and her control cracked. "You think you have it so bad but you wanna know what a crap family is? You wanna know what a dump is? Being left alone for two days when you're ten because your parents forgot to get a babysitter, or having to clean up their vomit when they got too drunk at the party they were hosting, or digging your dinner out of the garbage can because your parents couldn't be bothered to feed you. That's crap!"

Ella's eyes went wide and Blake swallowed back more words. The girl didn't know what Blake's life had been like growing up; she probably couldn't even comprehend such a thing.

Looking down, Ella flipped her phone over in her hands. "Well, if you didn't lose it, then where did all of Dad's money go?" She looked up, a challenge in her eyes.

Blake opened her mouth but the truth stuck to her tongue. She would see the pain in Ella's eyes, the hurt, the anger. How could she destroy the memories of her father?

"I... I don't know," she lied. "I only know that it's gone."

Ella's eyes narrowed. "You're lying." As she stormed away she yelled, "You're always lying!"

Unable to sleep, Blake rolled back and forth. She checked her phone. 12:26am. Sighing, she closed her eyes but after what felt like eternity, she grabbed her phone. 1:03am.

She pulled up Cam's name in her text messages. She read through them... again. They always made her smile.

Chewing her lip, she debated. It was one in the morning. He was probably asleep like a sane person. If he wasn't, would he think her crazy for texting him? If he was asleep and saw her message in the morning, he'd probably still think that.

Her fingers hovered over the buttons. Technically, he had texted her last, so it was her turn... right?

Did texting him make her seem needy? Lonely? Desperate?

Maybe she was all of those things. Heart racing, she typed.

Blake: Hey, you awake?

She paused, staring at the send button. She was actually sweating. This was stupid. She shouldn't be texting him at this hour. Or at all. Probably. Maybe?

Blake blew out a breath and pushed send. She flopped onto her back and turned the phone off, laying it on her chest. She would not stare at the screen while she waited for her heart to stop pounding.

Her phone vibrated and her eyes shot open.

Cam: I'm a serial killer. What do you think?

She felt a stupid grin spread across her face.

Cam: Why r u still awake?

Blake: Catwoman, remember?

She burrowed deeper into her blankets, smiling like an idiot. At least there was no one here to witness it.

Cam: Ooooohhh, right. Right. A nightprowler. Wait... r u following me? R u like a vigilante catwoman?

Blake: Been tailing you for hours.

Cam: That explains the odd feeling of being watched.

Cam: Gasp, are you wearing black leather now???

She laughed.

Blake: Wouldn't you like to know.

Cam: Maybe I would. Although, I rather liked the Wonder Woman attire you were sporting the first time we met.

Blake stared at their conversation, her smile fading. What was she thinking? Her life was a mess–she couldn't be in a relationship right now. Not that Cam indicated he wanted one. Aside from his incessant flirting, he'd never asked her out... almost as if he knew she would say no.

She couldn't right now anyway, not with everything going on. Not while things were so hard with Ella.

Cam: Are you alright?

While she debated how truthfully she should answer, he texted again.

Cam: Sorry, that was a stupid question. How about this? How can I help?

Blake stared at her screen. Was he for real? Why was he always giving without demanding some sort of compensation? Maybe she just didn't know him well enough yet to have found something about him she didn't like. Maybe he left dirty socks everywhere. Maybe he snored really loud. Maybe he left toenail clippings on the floor.

Blake: It's okay. Life is just dumb sometimes.

Cam: It really can be.

Suddenly, she felt incredibly stupid and insecure.

Blake: Sorry I bothered you, I know it's late.

Cam: You're not a bother and I'm glad you texted. Even if I was actually asleep, it still wouldn't have bothered me.

The corner of her mouth lifted just a little.

Blake: Well, you should probably sleep.

Cam: Me? What about you? Oh wait... you probably catnap all day.

She huffed out a laugh, feeling better and lame all at the same time.

Blake: Goodnight Cam.

Cam: Hey, you're doing amazing. Try to remember that. Try to believe that.

Cam: Text anytime. Night.

* * *

"I am not making these for Cam," Blake muttered as she mixed the butter and sugar together. "*I* want cookies, therefore, *I* am making them."

She still felt silly after texting him last night and even more ridiculous for crying on him the other day, so the man had earned cookies... even though she was absolutely not making them as an excuse to see him. She didn't want to see him. She was too embarrassed.

Blake glanced over her shoulder to where Ella and Brook had destroyed the living room. Dresses, fabric, ribbons, lace, and shoes were strewn everywhere.

She was grateful that at least one of Ella's friends hadn't turned their back on her when they had to sell the house and move. Brook seemed to bring out Ella's good side–or rather, her old self.

Smiling as the girls giggled and looked through fashion photos online, Blake dug around for the baking soda. "I'm making them for us girls, *not* Cam," she said, almost convincing herself. "Hey, Ella? Where's the baking soda?"

"I don't know," Ella called back. "I haven't seen any."

Blake put her hands on her hips. "Crap." Of course she would be out of something. Why hadn't she bothered to check if she had all the ingredients before making them?

Maybe Cam had some. Maybe he wasn't home, even though she knew he was because she'd heard his door open and close about an hour ago. Maybe she should just go to the store. Maybe—

"Oh, for pete's sake," she muttered, and marched out of her apartment. Blake knocked on Cam's door before she could overthink things anymore. She was driving herself crazy.

"Just a second," Cam's voice called from somewhere inside.

The door opened.

"Hey, Cam. I—" Her words cut off as he pulled the door open all the way. He was in a pair of dark blue sweats, a towel hanging around the back of his neck.

No shirt. She tried not to stare at the broad chest and muscled arms and shoulders but, dang. She forced her eyes up to the wet hair that stuck to his forehead. She swallowed, catching the scent of his freshly applied deodorant.

His mouth turned up into a lopsided grin. "Cat got your tongue?"

She rolled her eyes. "Don't you dare start with the cat puns."

He laughed. "Come in. I'll just grab a shirt."

She almost thanked him but decided that sounded insulting. Still, she was glad. She didn't need to be distracted like that.

Lucifer was perched on the window sill and she went over to pet him.

Cam returned in a tight white t-shirt. Well, crap. That wasn't much better.

"What's up?" he asked.

"Um, I'm making cookies and apparently don't have any more baking soda."

Cam smiled. "If I give you the baking soda does it earn me a cookie?"

Blake pretended to consider it. "I guess that's fair."

"So are you an eat-the-dough kind of girl?" he asked while rummaging through a cupboard.

"Is that even a question?" Blake replied, making sure she looked horrified. "Who doesn't like cookie dough?"

Cam shrugged. "There are some questionable characters out there who seem to think it's bad for you or something."

"Pish, amateurs," Blake muttered, earning a laugh from him.

"I swear," Cam muttered, watching Blake stroke Lucifer's fur. "You're the only person he likes." He leaned toward the cat. "What did I ever do to you?"

It hissed at him, making Cam scrunch his nose. He handed over the baking soda.

"Thanks," Blake said, accepting it.

"Anytime," he said. He interlocked his fingers and rocked back on his heels. "Hey, I have a favor to ask."

Blake stiffened, bracing for what he would say. She couldn't help it. She'd had too many experiences where what had appeared to be kindness turned into tally marks that the other person wanted compensation for.

"My sister's birthday is coming up and I'd like to get her something fun. She loves antiques and there's a flea market across town." His cheeks seemed to redden just a bit. "I was just getting ready to go and, I know it's pretty last minute so I get that you probably can't but, if you and Ella happen to be free, would you be willing to come with me?"

Whatever Blake had expected him to say, *that* wasn't it. It sounded... completely fun.

"Um, well, we have Brook over right now. I don't know how you feel about another tagalong."

Cam shrugged. "I'm sure it would be more fun for Ella to bring a friend."

35

"Wait," Blake said, narrowing her eyes and leaning forward. "Is this one of your serial killer tricks?"

Cam held up his hands. "I wouldn't dare take on Catwoman." A mischievous glint appeared in his eyes. "Or Wonder Woman."

Blake almost swatted him but decided that would come off as too flirtatious. Instead, she gave him a giant smile then hurried back to her apartment and asked Ella and Brook about going. At first, Ella acted uninterested but Brook convinced her, saying they might find something cool for Prom.

Soon, the four of them stood at the elevator, the girls laughing over something on their phones. When the elevator slid open, Wyatt stood there, wearing his Grand Duke's Repair Service shirt.

"Hey, Wyatt," Cam said cheerfully as they entered.

The man nodded. "Cam." Wyatt watched them from the corner of his eye, taking in the three-to-one ratio.

The doors closed and after a moment, Cam cracked his knuckles, making Wyatt jump.

"Coming from Mr. King's place again?"

Wyatt straightened his glasses. "Mmm hmm."

There was a beat of silence, then Cam leaned close to Blake. "When we're done, I know this great spot in the woods. Quiet, remote. So remote that even if you were to scream, no one would hear you."

The elevator dinged and Wyatt all but flew out, banging his tool box against the wall. He cast a slightly terrified look over his shoulder as he scuttled from the building.

As soon as he was out of earshot, Blake and Cam burst into laughter.

"Oh my gosh," Blake wheezed. "You are so bad!"

Cam wiped tears from his eyes. "I know, I shouldn't have done that."

They looked at each other, then started laughing all over again.

Ella just shook her head. "Old people are so weird."

Seven

T he flea market filled the parking lot beside an old movie theater that had gone out of business ages ago. Pop-up canopies, booths, and tables were set out in rows. Blake smiled when Ella and Brook squealed, dashing off together to investigate all the vendor stations.

"That's the happiest I've seen her in, well, a long time," Blake said. "Thanks for inviting us."

Cam shrugged. "You're doing me the favor, remember?"

She gave him a yeah-right look. "Somehow I doubt that."

They meandered through the market together, all the while Cam making her laugh. It felt so natural to be with him that she found herself relaxing, even being silly. Anytime she'd gone somewhere with Warren, it was somewhere fancy. Galas, dinner meetings, award ceremonies. She was always dressed in fancy clothes and sparkling jewelry. She'd loved it at the time. It was like getting to play dress-up and be the princess. But even as she'd sold it all, she found she didn't miss it. She was much more comfortable here.

"Can I ask you something personal?" Blake asked.

Cam gave her a worried look. "I will not give away any of my trade secrets. The nightstand market is far too crowded as it is." He looked thoughtful. "Maybe it is time I move on to pinky toes."

Dang, her face hurt from smiling so much. "You seem like a good guy, aside from the, yanno—" She made a stabbing motion " —part."

He laughed.

"How is it you're not married?" She leaned closer, making a show of concern that they would be overheard. "Do you leave toenail clippings on the floor?"

Cam smiled, but his eyes seemed to lose some of their luster. Maybe she shouldn't have asked but she needed to know.

"I was engaged once," he said.

She raised her brows but said nothing, waiting for him to continue.

"I was going to law school at the time," Cam said, stopping to admire the display of geodes. "Studying corporate law. I was on track to get an internship with one of those snotty law firms that handle high profile cases and make lots of money." He wiggled his eyebrows.

She sighed dramatically. "From lawyer to killer, a tale as old as time."

Cam had to pause while he held his side and laughed. "I started dating a girl from school. She and I were in some of the same classes. She was from a prominent family, dedicated and driven. She even set up a great job interview for me after graduation in her hometown. Eventually I proposed."

Blake eyed him thoughtfully.

"What? he asked.

"I dunno... I'm having a hard time picturing you as a lawyer."

His mouth quirked up into that lopsided smile she was really starting to love. "Wait until we get into a debate about something." Then his smile faded. "Then Steven died. After that, my ambitions just didn't seem to matter like they used to. I wanted to stay closer to home and do something that allowed me to see my family often. I didn't want to spend the extra time in law school trying to finish a law degree I wouldn't use. I needed to be able to help with the ranch, so I pulled back and became an accountant."

Blake stopped dead in her tracks. "Wait. You're an accountant?"

Cam's confident expression faltered. "Do you think that's bad?"

"What? No! I just assumed you were a pilates instructor or something."

He made a face.

She grinned. "Sorry. There's absolutely nothing wrong with being an accountant. It's just that the word always conjures up images of guys with glasses and comb overs."

Cam touched his hair, his eyes wide with fear as if it would disappear right then and there. Then he laughed. "I suppose it does. But I like numbers. They make sense to me." He shoved his hands into his pockets and shrugged. "When I told my fiance that I was quitting law school and wanted to stay here, we just couldn't work past that. So she left."

"Oh," Blake said. "I'm so sorry."

"Eh, it's for the best," he said, but she could feel his sadness. "I mean, I was a mess for a long time. Being home helped, though, even if it wasn't the same without Steven."

She thought about how hard that must have been, losing two people you loved so close together in such different ways. Glancing at Cam, she couldn't help but think that his ex really missed out on something special.

"Oh, you should taste these," Cam said, placing a hand on her lower back to gently guide her toward a booth of goat cheese. Blake shivered, liking the feel of his hand there. It made her feel safe, like she was precious and wanted, and maybe... that he liked touching her.

As they meandered, he would often do that, softly touch the sensitive spot on her lower back when he wanted to focus her attention somewhere. Blake found herself reaching for his arm, pulling him to a stop so she could show him something that caught her eye.

Up ahead, Blake caught sight of a station that had several sets of old fashioned clocks, cameras, and even a typewriter. She gasped, grabbing Cam's hand as she pulled him over. "Look at all these!" She inspected the clocks and was eventually drawn to the typewriter. "This is so cool," she said, running the fingers of her free hand over its keys. She really loved it. Warren's house was pristine, everything new and shiny looking. Deep down, Blake had always been more of a shabby chic kind of girl.

"You like it?" Cam asked from behind her. She turned. He was looking at their grasped hands.

"It's amazing," Blake said, unsure if she was talking about a typewriter or the feel of Cam's fingers laced with hers. Suddenly self-conscious, she pulled free and moved to look at the other pieces but eventually came back to the beautifully preserved machine. She discreetly checked the price tag and cringed. She certainly wouldn't be buying it. With a twinge of sadness, she added, "I bet your sister would love it if she likes antiques. Or, if she already has one, this clock is really cool." She picked up a dark mantle clock with gold filigree designs. She looked up to find Cam watching her.

"What?" she asked.

He shrugged, shifting closer. "Nothing, You're just cute when you get excited."

Blake stilled, wishing she had the courage to reach for his hand again. He closed the space between them.

"It's perfect," Cam said, reaching to take it from her. His fingers brushed over hers, in a very deliberate way, his eyes still on her face. "Thanks."

Blake swallowed, not moving. She didn't want to. She loved the way he made her laugh, loved that he didn't seem to mind her life was a dumpster fire, loved that he seemed so genuinely good. All of that made her love being with him and... she liked who she was with him.

"If you buy two clocks," the vendor said, breaking the spell and making them break apart. "I'll give you a very good deal."

Blake's heart raced and it took a moment to calm her breath. While Cam paid the vendor, she texted Ella, asking where she was. When she looked up, she caught a woman watching her. Blake squinted. She seemed vaguely familiar, but before she could place her, the woman turned and disappeared into the crowd.

They found Ella and Brook talking to two boys by an ice cream stand. Blake recognized them from the band. Jack and Gus.

Jack handed Ella a cone and he grinned when she sank her teeth into it, only to make a face as the cold treat touched them. Ella didn't flirt with Jack the way she did with Prince, but oh man, this boy had it bad for her.

Brook saw them first and waved. Ella ran over. "We're going to stay longer. Jack said he could bring us home after."

Blake looked between the two girls, then back to the boys. "Are you asking me or telling me?" It was becoming a common phrase between them. Blake hardly knew a dang thing about parenting, but she did know she needed to establish some boundaries, especially because Ella kept trying to knock them all down.

Ella's smile was replaced with a scowl. "*Can* we stay longer?" she ground out.

"Brook needs to check with her parents first. If she can stay, then you can too. But you girls need to stay together."

Ella rolled her eyes. Brook was already texting her folks. "I can stay but my mom is going to pick me up at seven," Brook said a minute later.

"Jack?" Blake called, and the two boys hurried over.

"Yes, Mrs. Johnston?"

"Have the girls back by six, please."

"Yes ma'am," Jack said, looking at Ella. He was so happy and she was so unaware.

The four teenagers moved away and Cam and Blake walked back towards the truck. She didn't pull away when Cam reached for her hand while saying something about when he was a teenager, but she missed it. All she could think about was how much she liked her hand in his.

When they reached his truck, a smoldering cigarette butt still burned on the ground by wheel. Cam kicked it away.

"Is there anything you need to do while we're out?" he asked as he opened the door for her.

Blake hoisted herself inside. "I just need to stop by and check on my storage unit, but you don't need to come. I'll just go after you drop me off."

"I can take you, if you don't mind me tagging along," he said, and Blake found she wanted him to come.

"Alright."

The Lock Box Storage Units was an outdoor storage facility. Nothing fancy, but clean and seemed to have decent surveillance.

"This one's mine," Blake said, stopping outside of unit sixty-four. She stared at it, but nothing seemed amiss. She'd already filled Cam in on what had happened.

"Did they say if the intruders tried to pick the lock?" Cam asked, inspecting it for signs of tampering.

Blake pulled out her key. "No, just that someone tried to open it. I guess I don't know what that means exactly." The lock clicked open and Cam pushed the door up.

She cringed. She'd forgotten how big the unit was and how full it looked. There was no way she could get rid of it. Ella would want a lot of this stuff when she was old enough to have a place of her own. Her dad's old desk, boxes and boxes of books from his office, his armchair, a hope chest, and half a dozen other things filled with memories.

The most she could hope for was to go through the boxes of papers and clothes and try to empty it enough to move the rest to a smaller unit and save a few dollars a month.

"You okay?" Cam asked softly.

She nodded, blowing out a long breath and forcing herself not to freak out. She would not be overwhelmed. Small steps. Small steps.

Blake walked to a box and lifted the lid, staring down at the papers piled inside. "I need to go through everything. Save what needs to be saved and get rid of the rest so I can downsize my unit."

She slumped over the box. "This is going to take forever."

Cam set a hand on her shoulder and she straightened. "How can I help?"

Dang it! He was so freaking nice. She shouldn't get used to depending on people, but she had to admit, it would be helpful to get some of these boxes out of here.

Small steps. Small steps.

"I'll give you my whole batch of cookie dough if you would be willing to haul a load of these boxes back to my apartment," she offered, cringing a little at how unfair it sounded.

Cam scratched his chin. "Half the cookie dough to be eaten together while we go through the boxes?"

Blake blinked. "Wait, you want to help me go through this stuff?"

He held up a hand, sighing dramatically. "You drive a hard bargain. Fine, I'll bring dinner and we'll have cookie dough while going through the boxes."

"But—" She was quite literally at a loss for words.

Cam picked up a piece of paper from the top and looked at it. "I'm an accountant and this has lots of numbers on it. I'm good with those, remember? I might be able to help determine if something needs to be kept or not."

Blake swallowed. Crap. He was going to make her cry *again*.

She should say no. There were no doubts that she could do this on her own, but she couldn't deny it would go so much faster with help. Clearing her throat to keep it from tightening too much, she said, "I suppose I shall *allow* your assistance. Since you're bringing dinner." She gave him a look that hopefully conveyed how ridiculous it was that he was offering so much to help *her*.

He pumped his fist. "You had me worried! I thought I would have to beg for that dough. I would do anything for cookie dough."

She arched an eyebrow. "Wait. You were going to beg? I take back my offer. I want you to beg—"

"No take-backs," Cam growled as he picked up a couple boxes and started carrying them towards his trucks.

Laughing, Blake followed.

A couple hours later, nacho boxes littered the counter, and papers covered the kitchen table.

Blake pretty much gave the stuff that looked important or business-y to Cam and she went through everything else.

She studied him now and the deep scowl that had been on his face for a long time. He compared a few papers, stacking some and pulling out others.

He blew out a sharp breath and looked up at her.

Cold wrapped around her chest. "What's wrong?"

His mouth thinned into a tight line, then he held up two pieces of paper. She stared at them. They looked identical but she had no idea what she was looking at.

"Can you spot the differences? Look at the numbers in the left column."

Blake squinted, her gaze jumping back and forth between the numbers. Finally, she spotted something. "That number has an extra zero." She kept looking. "And those two numbers are switched." She looked at Cam. "What does that mean?"

He lowered the papers. "It means someone was embezzling money, and I don't think it was your husband."

eight

B lake stared out her window. The only noise in the apartment was Ella's chatter as she talked with Brook on the phone.

Her thoughts were still in chaos. The past week had been like walking through a hurricane, dealing with work, police, phone calls, lawyers, and Ella, and now she was standing in the eye of it, waiting in the calm. Waiting, waiting, until she was pushed back into the roaring wind.

Blake thought about the two women who'd worked for Warren. Anna was his secretary and Zelle was his finance clerk. They had both seemed nice enough, though a little distant. Still, he'd invited them to attend their wedding ceremony.

When the police looked deeper into them, they discovered they were sisters who'd changed their last names. How had she not noticed the similarities between them?

They were women who'd sunk other companies before. Sisters who ran long cons.

They were the ones who had embezzled money from the company, sinking it. The police were now investigating the gambling debts. It was believed that Anna and Zelle Tramaine used or forged Warren's name and so the debt was not Warren's, but theirs.

She shook her head as if to clear it. If that were the case, Blake would no longer be responsible for it all. Just the thought should have made her feel better, like a huge weight was going to be lifted from her shoulders, but she stubbornly held on to it. Part of her couldn't believe that it would work out that way. If it didn't, she wouldn't be able to handle the crushing devastation.

She glanced at Ella. Blake still hadn't told her anything; she didn't want to until she knew for *sure*. No question. She didn't want to take the news to her and explain everything, only to have to retract it later. But… that's what Warren had done with his cancer. Waited and waited until it was too late. Maybe it was time to stop waiting. Maybe it was time to just be honest.

There was a soft knock on her door. She turned away from staring at the cars parked along the street, and the woman who sat smoking in the old black car. She'd been there almost every day.

Maybe she lived in her vehicle.

Blake went to the door and looked through the peephole.

Cam.

Her heart immediately reacted, beating harder and hotter. She hesitated for a moment. She was still in sweats, her hair pulled into a messy bun. No makeup.

Then, she shrugged. She'd tried being perfect for people before. Didn't change anything, just made her feel worse about herself. Blake was too emotionally tired for all that now. Letting out a sharp breath, she opened the door.

Cam's face split into a wide smile, his gaze moving over her face like a caress. "Beautiful," he said, almost as if to himself.

Her eyebrows shot up. That was the last thing she'd expected him to say.

He blinked. "Hey."

Despite herself, Blake's mouth quirked up on one side. "Hey."

Cam shifted the box in his hands. "I have a special delivery for Catwoman. Or, Wonder Woman, whoever happens to be home right now."

She huffed out a small laugh and held the door open wider. "Come in."

He slipped past her and Blake caught a whiff of his cologne. She shivered, goosebumps shooting down her arms. She wanted that scent to wrap around her and never leave. Cam set the box on the counter with a soft *thunk*.

"What in the world," Blake asked, staring at it. "What is it?"

Cam looked completely horrified. "I can't tell you that! You have to open it."

Blake just stood there. It's not that she'd never been given a gift before. Warren gave her stuff all the time, but then again, money was never a problem. Somehow this felt different, though she wasn't sure why.

Cam moved up behind her and set a hand on her hip. A jolt of warmth shot through her at the contact, making her want to lean back into him.

"It won't bite," he teased, his whispered words in her ear making her core melt. "I promise." He removed his hand and stepped away. She wished he'd come back.

Slowly, Blake pulled back the cardboard flaps and peered inside. Her throat closed as emotions pushed up from her chest.

"You… got me the typewriter?" she asked in a whisper as she ran her fingers over the keys.

He shrugged. "I thought it might cheer you up. You've seemed pretty run-down these last few days."

She smirked to cover the emotion still building in her chest. "I'm just not wearing makeup."

Cam's face lost any trace of teasing. "Your face is... perfection."

His words, spoken so plainly with no expectations attached, impacted her more deeply than she wanted to admit.

"I..." She swallowed hard and cleared her throat. "Thank you for the gift. I don't know what to say. These last few days have been crazy, but I hope you know how grateful I am for everything you've done. Everything you've helped with. I—"

"Blake?" Cam said, interrupting.

"Mmm?"

"You're welcome. Now, stop thanking me and tell me how you're doing. Really. Honestly."

She closed her mouth, having the strongest urge to hug the man and not let go for a long, long time. Instead, she wrapped her arms around herself to keep from reaching for him and leaned against the table. "I'm okay."

He arched his brows at her.

"Ish. Okay-ish," she amended. "I don't know, honestly. I feel... relieved. Scared." She looked down. "Lost." She huffed a laugh. "I know, I should be feeling better but I'm just not, and I don't know why."

"Lost?" he asked.

She shook her head then shrugged a shoulder. "Yeah." She peeked at him. "Can I ask you something?"

"Always," he said, turning so he too was leaning against the table. Their arms almost touched.

She swallowed, shifting so they did touch. He didn't pull away. "Do you... do you find it hard to let people in? Or rather, let people get close because you're afraid of them... leaving?"

He seemed to still beside her so she hurried to finish her thought. "This whole mess is... intense," she admitted. "It seems unreal, like a movie or something."

Cam inhaled, long and deep. "For a while, yes," he finally admitted. "It was hard to trust people, hard to believe I was liked for me and not for what I could do for them, or what they wanted me to be. I didn't want to get hurt again. I saw lies everywhere, I questioned whether people would be true to their word." He crossed his arms. "I pushed people away, didn't let anyone get too close. It was safer that way."

Blake nodded. He'd just described her whole life. In many ways it was all she knew... even with Warren. He was good to her, but the more she thought about it, she had to admit that she'd always held back just a little, afraid he'd change his mind and not want her. Afraid he'd leave.

He did, though admittedly not in the way she'd pictured.

"But I also found no happiness anywhere," he said, startling her. "The less I trusted, the more bitter I became. It was a very miserable way to live."

Blake shifted uncomfortably, suddenly wanting to change the subject but struggling to think of something to say. She stared at the wall, wishing she could lean against Cam and just breathe him in. Surely he couldn't be real. People were not this way in real life.

Cam pushed away from the table and faced her. "I need to tell you something."

She swallowed. Already her old fears of being left were creeping back in.

"About a week before you moved in, I had decided I was going to move back to the ranch. I can work remotely so it wouldn't be a problem."

His words tore through her, leaving a gaping hole in her chest. She blinked hard, swallowing down the hurt. Of course he was leaving. They always left her.

"Do you want me to stay, Blake?" he asked, his voice low. "Because I would stay. For you."

Her eyes shot to his, startled. His gaze was so intense she had to look away, still trying to absorb what he'd just said and what he'd just asked.

She didn't look up from his chest, even as he moved closer to her. Her breath came faster, her heart pulsed, pounded, raced. Yes, she wanted him to stay. Yes, she wanted to know if he was really... him. Wanted to know if he would keep her.

She gripped her arms as he stood close enough to feel his breath in her hair.

Slowly, he reached for one of her hands. She had to let go of her arm so he could take it, drawing it to his chest.

"Would you want me to stay?" he asked.

Her stomach was in knots, aching from the desire to reach for him, but fear held her still. What if, later, he decided he didn't want her after all? It surprised her how much that actually hurt to think about.

"Ask. Me," he whispered.

This time her gaze was slow as it rose to meet his. His eyes were warm, almost pleading, making her walls crumble. Reflexively, she tried to hold those walls in place. Cam choosing her felt too... unreal.

"Ask me to stay, Blake," he said again, rubbing his thumb over her knuckles, heating her from the inside out.

Her mouth parted. The words were there, wanting to be said.

A squeal from Ella startled them both and Cam turned. Blake slipped her hand free of his and inhaled sharply, trying to calm her racing heart.

"Blake!" Ella bounded into the room. "I want to do this for prom." She held up her phone, showing a girl with blonde hair that had soft pink highlights. "We can just get temporary dye. It would match my dress and be *so* cute!"

Blake looked into her stepdaughter's bright blue eyes, trying to shift from her conversation with Cam to this moment with Ella. "Definitely! It will be amazing! Do you still need help with your dress?"

"Nope. Don't need your help," Ella said.

Her blatant dismissiveness hurt, but Blake was quick to hide it because Ella was already twirling away.

"Next Saturday can't come fast enough," Ella called over her shoulder as she ran back over to Brook.

Slowly, Blake turned back to Cam, afraid she'd see hurt or anger in his eyes. Or worse, see that he'd finally given up on her. Instead, his eyes were soft and there was a little smile on his lips.

"Take your time," he said, giving her arm a squeeze. "I'm not exactly far away." He winked then walked out her front door.

Blake was frozen in place. She'd learned quite young that you didn't ask for things you wanted, didn't beg for anything from anyone, but for the first time in a long time, she wanted to ask. She wanted Cam to stay, but the fear of rejection owned her, rooting her feet in place as the door closed behind him.

Nine

Blake pressed the up button to call the elevator, groaning from the effort it seemed to take. She'd been signing up to cover shifts as often as she could whenever they came available but today had taken longer than usual. No, today was ridiculous. She'd met a lot of picky people in her time, particularly among the upper class, but her last house of the day took the cake. Who ironed their socks and dish towels anyway?

The door dinged open revealing Wyatt. He was in jeans this time, making him look more human.

She moved aside so he could exit the elevator. "Hey, Wyatt," she managed.

"Blake," he said, with more vocal intonation than she was used to hearing from him.

They switched spots. He looked about to say something, paused, then said, "It's good to see you—"

The elevator doors slid shut but she managed to catch his last words.

"Still breathing."

She chuckled, thinking of Cam. He hadn't brought up their conversation about him staying, as though he knew she just needed a bit of space to absorb it all.

They had gotten good at coming up with completely ridiculous excuses to see each other every day. She needed him to get something off a shelf she was perfectly capable of reaching. Lucifer missed her. She couldn't find her shoe. He didn't know how to make toast.

He'd even insisted she store the stuff she still needed to go through from storage in his spare room until she could downsize to a smaller unit. All the document boxes had already been turned over to the police.

She grinned at Cam's door. He had to run out to his parent's ranch but said he'd come by after to "check if the water from her faucet was watery enough to drink." Laughing to herself, Blake opened her door, ready for some sweat pants and junk food.

"Hey, Ella," she said to the mound of blankets on the couch as she set her purse and bag with the pink hair dye onto the counter. The mound didn't move. The TV played some kind of dramatically romantic movie. On the floor beside the furniture was an opened bag of chocolate, the peanut butter jar with a spoon sticking out of it, and their last bag of chips.

"Ella?" she said again, moving into the living room.

That's when she noticed the roll of toilet paper and the tiny mountain of used tissues.

The mound on the couch sniffed.

Blake's heart sank. She crouched down beside Ella, fighting for calm. The face that barely poked out from under the blankets was red and puffy.

"Ella, what's wrong? What happened?"

Finally, the girl stirred, taking her eyes from the TV screen to look at Blake. She sniffed again and held out her phone. "Someone sent this to me," she whispered.

Blake took the phone, dreading what she would find. She pushed play on the video. There was Prince, his arm thrown over the shoulder of a pretty blonde.

Huh. Apparently, he had a type.

They both smiled and laughed and then Prince turned to the girl and kissed her. And... kissed her. Blake wrinkled her nose as the two teens continued to make out.

"She's a senior from another high school," Ella said, her voice still small. "They met a few days after Prince asked me to prom."

"Oh, Ella. I'm so sorry," Blake said, her heart breaking for Ella.

Ella stared at the TV for a while. "He asked one of his friends to take the video so it could *accidentally* find its way to me. He wants to take her to Prom, not me."

Blake had to grind her teeth to keep from saying something completely juvenile and inappropriate.

She could say the cliche' stuff such as, "his loss," and, "forget about him, you'll find someone better." But those words would feel hollow to her right now..

"You should still go," Blake said.

Ella looked away from the TV and blinked at her. "What?"

"You should still go to Prom. I'll get tickets for you and Brook. You girls can go together, have a blast, and show him that you don't need him, that your self esteem is not something he can take away from you. That you are not the kind of girl to lay on the couch all night weeping over him."

Ella shook her head. "I don't know."

"Life isn't fair," she said, knowing she sounded like an old person attempting to spout something inspirational but sounding like a moron instead. "It will never be fair. People can be cruel, but your value does not come from what other people think of you. You are of worth simply because... you *are*." She brushed hair from Ella's eyes.

"No one who makes you feel like less is worthy of your tears. No one who intentionally hurts you is worth your heart. Someday, you will find someone who makes you feel safe and loved simply because of who they are, and they will cherish everything about you."

Blake's heart raced, thinking of Cam. She needed to take a chance. She *wanted* to take a chance. She *wanted* to ask Cam to stay.

Touching her forehead to Ella's, she added, "Until then, be strong, and love yourself."

Ella was silent for a long moment. "Laying it on a little thick, aren'tcha?"

Blake laughed. "I don't know what you mean. I thought my speech was completely riveting and rather profound."

"You said cheesy wrong," Ella said, but there was a small smile on her lips.

Blake shrugged. "I like cheese."

This time, Ella did roll her eyes.

"What do you say, kiddo?" Blake asked, rubbing the girl's back. "Wanna dress up and go to a dance with your best friend?"

A small fire ignited in Ella's eyes. "You know what? I think I do."

Blake couldn't stop the wide smile from spreading across her face. "Good girl."

* * *

Blake raced through the shift she'd agreed to cover, anxious to get home. Ella would be getting ready for prom by herself. Brook could go with her, but her mom wouldn't be able to drop her off until just a little bit before it started.

She'd texted Ella to let her know she was on her way home but Ella never responded.

Blake pulled into her parking spot, noting the black car and the woman who always sat inside. Maybe she should introduce herself, see if she really was living out of her vehicle.

Another time.

She ran to the elevator, bouncing on her feet, impatient for the doors to open.

Prom started in just over an hour.

"I'm here!" Blake yelled as soon as she opened her door. She ran to Ella's room only to find the door locked. "Ella?"

"This is a disaster!" Ella yelled from the other side. "I messed up. I messed it all up."

"What are you talking about?" Blake asked, shaking the knob. "Please let me in."

For a moment, Blake wasn't sure she would, but then the lock clicked and the door swung open.

Blake couldn't completely stop the shock from showing on her face. Ella's hair was fluorescent pink, not the soft pink she'd been hoping for. Her eyeliner was noticeably uneven, and the dress, that had been too big for her to begin with, was sloppy and uneven on her shoulders where she and Brook tried to hand sew it.

Blake hated the despair she saw in Ella. She should have bought her a dress. She could have insisted they look through the thrift stores, or she could have at least butted in and helped to fix her mother's dress, but Ella hadn't wanted her to. She had been too hurt, too upset.

Ella's eyes filled with frustrated tears. "I tried," she said. "I really did try."

Blake pulled her into a hug and to her surprise, Ella hugged her back. They stood there for a long minute, Blake's heart breaking and healing in the same moment.

Ella sniffed. "I'm sorry you wasted money on tickets. I know we can't really afford them." She pulled back. "Maybe you can get a refund?"

Blake racked her brain. There had to be something she could do! Her phone dinged loudly, surprising them. She didn't remember having her volume up that loud.

Mamie: Hey Blake! I was just thinking about you! I want you to know that I'm a bored old woman so if you ever need help with anything, LITERALLY ANYTHING, I'm here for you!

Blake looked at Ella. "I have an idea."

* * *

When Blake, Ella, and Brook pulled into the driveway of Mamie's massive house, Ella sank down into her seat. "Are you sure about this, Blake?"

Before she could answer, the front door opened and Mamie came out, moving swiftly to the passenger side in shiny red stilettos and a black flowing cape dress, and opened Ella's door.

She flinched, instinctively shrinking from Mamie, but the woman smiled. "I have just the thing to fix that," she said, touching Ella's hair.

Ella lifted her head. "Really?"

Mamie held out her hand. "Come on. We'll get you fixed up."

Ella hesitated then reached for the woman's hand.

Blake mouthed a thank you when Mamie looked at her. She winked.

In what seemed like minutes, Mamie had Ella's face clear of makeup and a special shampoo in her hair.

Blake could only stare as the woman worked. She moved without any hesitation, washing, drying, and curling Ella's hair until it fell in soft, pastel pink waves. She didn't seem the least bit tired when she started on Ella's makeup. While she worked, she prattled on about what it had been like when she went to prom and even managed to make Ella laugh with the tale of her first kiss.

Finally, Mamie pulled back. "That should do it."

She handed Ella a mirror.

Her whole body stilled as she stared, and stared, and stared. Blake's anxiety was going to be the end of her as she waited for Ella to turn around. When she did, Brook gasped.

"Wow! You look... amazing, Ella!"

She looked at Blake not Brook, a small smile on her lips. "Yeah?"

For the first time since Warren's death, Blake saw Ella's vulnerability, her need to have the love of a parent, supporting her, uplifting her.

Blake took her hands. "You look so beautiful." And she meant it. Ella was completely stunning. "Your father would be so proud of who you are becoming. And so am I."

This time, Ella was the one who pulled Blake into a hug.

"Thank you," she whispered.

"Here we are," Mamie said, breaking the spell. She held up a long, pale blue dress that sparkled like it held all the stars in the night sky.

Ella's eyes were wide as she reached for the dress, then drew her hands back. "Are you sure?"

Mamie beamed at her. "Absolutely." She held up a finger. "And for the final touch..." she bent and picked up a box. "Shoes really do make the outfit." She lifted the lid and all the girls gasped.

The shoes looked iridescent as the older woman pulled them from the box. The shimmery fabric of the thick-soled tennis shoe was sheer, like the fairy's wings one reads about in fantasy books.

Reverently, Ella accepted the shoes and slid them, tying the bright white laces. "They fit perfectly," Ella said, standing and twirling.

Blake smiled. She really did look like a princess from a fairytale.

"I'll have my chauffeur take you girls in the red car," Mamie said with a wink.

With a final wave, the girls squealed as they ran out to the flashy red sports car Mamie had sent for.

As soon as they were gone, Blake grabbed Mamie's hand. "I don't know how to begin to thank you."

Mamie squeezed back. "Nonsense. I haven't had this much fun in ages. Truly.

It was the perfect gift to me." She raised her eyebrows. "Now, isn't there something you need to take care of tonight? Someone you need to talk to? Maybe say how you really feel?"

Blake tilted her head, staring at this woman who came into her life just when she had needed her the most.

Mamie's smile faltered. "You love him, don't you?"

Heat flushed through Blake at the word love, but yes, she did. She loved the way his eyes crinkled in the corners, and the way her face always hurt from smiling when he was around. She loved the way he never judged her for struggling, or made her feel incapable, even though he was always helping her out. She loved the way she felt curled against his broad chest, and the way his skin felt so right against her own.

Mamie winked. "Go talk to him."

"Yes. Yes, I need to go. Thank you so much. For everything," Blake said as Mamie pulled her into a quick tight hug. Blake hurried back to her car while texting Cam.

Blake: Hey, are you home?

She set her phone in the middle console and headed back to the apartment. She kept checking the screen but there was no follow up text.

Chewing her lip, she tried to not let her mind wander down dark paths. He was just busy or away from his phone. He wasn't avoiding her, he hadn't done that so far, so why would he do it now? Unless he was tired of waiting—

"Stop it, Blake!" she ground out, gripping the steering wheel. She just needed to get home. When she did she would knock on his door, then call him. Or, use the key and "check on Lucifer." Did that make her look desperate? Probably.

Blake parked then rushed into the building, racing to the elevator. She pushed the button. Then pushed it again. And again. And again. And again.

It dinged open and she almost ran straight into Wyatt, who was no doubt coming from fixing yet another thing in Mr. King's apartment.

"Oh! I'm so sorry," she said, skirting around him.

Wyatt straightened his glasses, maneuvering around her too. "No problem. Oh, hey, someone was looking for—"

The doors slid shut.

Ten

Blake checked her phone just as the battery gave up and died. Cam still hadn't replied. She walked straight to his door and knocked, afraid if she went home first, she'd lose her nerve. Not that she was unsure of her decision, but rather, not knowing if she had waited too long. The only sounds were her own breaths as she stood there. Nothing. He wasn't home.

That's fine, she would call him once she could get her phone plugged in. Blake moved to her own apartment and unlocked the door, only barely registering the rather strong smell of cigarette smoke.

Blake pushed open her door and moved to set her purse and keys on the counter. She froze, staring at the apartment. Books and papers littered the floor, drawers had been emptied and cast aside, couch cushions had been tossed from their place.

"What—"

Something pressed into her back. "Don't move," a voice hissed in her ear, the woman's breath heavy with stale smoke.

Blake's heart stuttered, her pulse racing. "What do you want?" she managed to say, her voice a little too high.

The woman moved to stand in front of her and for a heart-stuttering moment, Blake could only stare at the small handgun pointed at her, feeling as though she was submerged in icy water. Then, she looked at the woman's face and blinked. "Anna?"

Anna was a tall woman with a round nose and thin lips. But since the time Blake had last seen her as Warren's secretary with long brown hair, it had since been dyed a garish shade of red and cut rather like a mullet.

ON BROKEN GLASS

Anna sneered down at Blake. "Where are all of Warren's things?"

"What? I—"

"If you want your boyfriend to live, tell me where Warren's things are."

Blake's stomach knotted painfully, making her want to vomit. At the same time, anger sparked in her chest. Cam. Her eyes narrowed. "If you hurt him—"

Anna snorted. "Just give me what I want and then you'll never see me again. I just need a small red booklet. Warren took it home by mistake his last week at the office. I need it."

Blake's thoughts were struggling to keep up. "A red notebook? I... I don't know. The police have the boxes from his home office, the rest is—"

She cut off abruptly.

Anna grinned, showing her grayish yellow teeth. "In your boyfriend's apartment. We know. Zelle is there looking for it now."

"Where's Cam? What did you do to him?" Blake demanded even as fear clawed it way up her chest.

"Nothing... yet." Anna's eyes glinted. "Where is the notebook?"

Blake fisted her shaking hands. "I don't know. I swear. I've never seen a red notebook. It might be in one of the boxes but—"

Anna waved her towards the door. "Then let's go see if it's there," she said, stepping closer. "If you try to scream or run, your boyfriend is dead."

Blake swallowed, and silently followed Anna's orders to enter Cam's apartment.

Inside, Cam was gagged and strapped to a kitchen chair with multiple zip ties. His eyes went wide when he saw her. Instinctively, Blake started towards him but Anna grabbed her shirt and pulled her back.

"I don't think so," she said, pressing the gun to Blake's side. Cam's eyes filled with so many emotions. With a muffled roar, he jerked his arm, snapping the two zip ties.

Before Anna could react, a small growl filled the air, followed by a loud hiss. Blake caught a flash of fur as Lucifer launched himself at Anna. She screamed, a shot firing into the wall before she dropped the gun to fight off the crazed cat, who clawed and bit her.

Ears ringing, Blake went to grab the gun, accidently kicking it away from her as she stumbled on shaking, unsteady legs.

Zelle ran into the living room, her long black hair pulled up into a wild bun. Her huge nose wrinkled as she looked from Blake to Anna, who was wrestling what no doubt appeared to be a rabid furball. Cam ripped away the rest of the zipties and tackled her.

Anna finally managed to throw Lucifer off her. Face scratched and bleeding, she spun to Blake, eyes wild. The woman reached for her, fingers out like claws, but Lucifer pounced on her again.

"Get my saran wrap," Cam yelled from the floor.

"What?" Blake asked, her feet feeling heavy as she stared at the mayhem around her.

"Next to the fridge," Cam yelled. "Second drawer!"

Blake finally moved, racing to the kitchen and grabbing the saran wrap from the drawer and tossing it to Cam, who had Zelle pinned to the ground.

Anna screamed, still struggling with Lucifer. She spun and ran straight into the wall, knocking herself out.

Lucifer hissed at her still form, then sat back on his haunches and proceeded to groom himself while somehow managing to look pleased.

"Let me go," Zelle screamed, bringing Blake's attention back to Cam, who had somehow managed to use the saran wrap like rope, tying the woman's hands and feet together behind her back.

"Whoa," Blake said, impressed. "That's actually really hot." It seemed ridiculous to feel that way in such a moment, but she did. Maybe she was in shock.

Cam looked up, grinning. "Rodeo."

Lucifer waltzed over to Zelle and smacked the woman in the face with his paw, over and over again while she tried to move her face out of the way.

Cam hurried to tie up Anna the same way he'd done with Zelle. He straightened and Blake could make out the sound of sirens in the distance.

Seeing him whole and unharmed made her shock melt away and she choked on a sob. She bolted toward him the same moment he moved towards her. They crashed into each other, Blake pressing her face into his neck. Tears escaped her eyes as his arms banded around her waist.

"You're alive," she whispered over and over again. Cam buried his hands into her hair, pressing her to his chest as though he was trying to absorb her into him.

"Are you okay?" he asked, pulling away to look at her, his eyes searching her for signs of injury.

She choked out a short laugh, nodding.

His hand slid to her face and his thumb brushed aside a tear. "When I saw that gun pointed at you—" He looked away for a moment, blinking rapidly as the muscles in his neck corded. "I wanted to rip her apart. I would have fought anything and anyone to get to you. I can't lose you, Blake."

Something in her heart seemed to click back together, as if a piece that had broken off long ago had found its place again. "You... you would fight for me?"

Cam's eyes grew so intense that Blake's breath caught in her throat.

"I would fight to keep you, always, as long as you wished it of me."

Blake quirked a brow. "Did you... did you just go all Jane Austin-y on me?"

A bit of that mischievous light that Blake had come to love returned to his gaze. "Is it working? Lucifer practically saved the day. I can't be outdone by a half-mad cat."

Blake laughed, she couldn't help it. They both did. There were too many emotions. Too fast. Too strong.

"Rodeo, huh?" she asked. "Can I see you in a cowboy hat?"

He leaned closer. "If I get to see you in black leather."

Instead of laughing, Blake gripped him tighter. "Stay," she blurted. Cam's smile faded.

The sirens were so close now, but she ignored them.

"Stay. With me," she whispered. "I'm not saying you have to stay here, like physically. I know you were going to go back to the ranch so maybe Ella and I could look at moving closer to you, unless you don't want us to do that, or unless you want to stay here, but maybe that's something we can—

Cam's mouth met hers, cutting off her flood of words.

His lips were warm, soft and searching, and as her mouth slowly responded to his, she could taste the salt of their tears. He pulled back slightly, as though giving her a chance to change her mind but she slipped her arms around his neck, pulling him back to her. Kissing him was like coming up for air after suffocating. How had she gone so long without breathing?

Eleven

Blake and Ella sat beside each other sharing a bag of potato chips. It had been a late night of getting looked over by EMT's, making statements to police, letting them search their apartments, and finally filling Ella in on all that had happened. They both fell asleep on Blake's bed before Ella got very far into the story about her prom night.

It was just after nine in the morning but they munched on the snacks they'd brought in with them last night.

"You okay?" Blake asked.

Ella bit into a chip. "Yeah. Just... a lot to process."

Blake nodded. "Yeah."

They chewed in silence for a while.

"I'm sorry," Ella said "about the way I've been behaving. It's not an excuse but I was just so mad. Mad at Dad, mostly, but I think it was just easier to direct it at you." She grabbed another chip. "I was so angry that he didn't tell me about the cancer sooner, and I kind of hated you because he told you and not me."

Blake nodded. "I know."

Ella looked at her. "You do?"

"I'm not saying I know how you're feeling," Blake clarified. "I just mean I know what it's like to be angry about life and the choices people make for you."

"For what it's worth," Ella said. "I'm glad Dad picked you."

Blake looked at her stepdaughter... no, her daughter. "Me too," she said, meaning it. Despite everything, she had come to love this girl. Genuinely.

A mischievous smile spread across Ella's face. "Should we talk about Cam? I mean, he is pretty cute."

Surprised, Blake's chip caught in her throat, making her cough so hard her eyes watered.

Ella just laughed.

Once they were both breathing normally again, Ella groaned. "I don't know how to tell Mamie I lost one of her shoes."

Blake turned onto her side. "How did that happen?"

Ella also turned so they were facing each other. "Brook and I were having so much fun and..." She picked at the blanket, trying to look sorry but failing. "I confess it felt pretty good to see Prince's eyes go as wide as golf balls when we walked in and then he practically stared at me all night. He made his date so mad she stormed out." Ella shrugged. "After that, Prince came up to me and asked me to dance. He tried to apologize but then started to get all handsy." She wrinkled her nose. "I pushed him away and told him never to touch me again but he wouldn't leave me alone. Finally, Jack grabbed him and pulled him away from me. My shoe fell off while I was trying to get away, and then I couldn't find it anywhere." She cringed. "Do you think Mamie will be mad?"

"I doubt it," Blake said, unfisting her hands that had tightened while Ella talked about Prince. "Even if she is, we'll figure it out. Let's get cleaned up and go over."

Ella nodded.

Blake scrunched her face. "Hey, do you know anything about a red notebook? Anna said your dad took hers by accident."

Ella thought for a moment, her eyes going wide. "Wait." She leapt out of bed and ran from the room. A minute later, she came back holding a small red notebook.

"I took a few things from Dad's office after—" She broke off and swallowed. "Well, I took a few things that I thought might have been some personal things. I remember looking through this and almost throwing it away cause I couldn't find anything interesting." She handed it to Blake, who flipped it open.

She'd looked at enough bank statements and account numbers in the last week to recognize what she was seeing. This had to be what Anna was looking for.

"Let's drop this off at the station on our way to Mamie's."

An hour later, Blake pulled into Mamie's driveway, surprised to see a for sale sign in the yard. Had that been there the night before? They rang the doorbell and someone Blake had never seen before opened it, smiling.

"Welcome. Are you here for the open house?"

Blake scrunched her brows. "Uh, no. We're here to see Mamie."

The woman clasped her hands together. "Mamie? I'm sorry. I don't know who that is."

"She's the lady who lives here," Blake clarified. Maybe she was just... new?

The woman laughed. "That's impossible. This house has been empty for months."

Blake and Ella looked at each other.

"But," Ella started. "We were here last night. We literally saw Mamie last night."

The woman looked back and forth between them. "Perhaps you have the wrong house?"

Blake pulled out her phone and called Mamie's number. It went straight to a generic voicemail, not the one where Mamie said to only leave a message if it's super important.

Not knowing what else to do, they left.

"How—" Ella started, looking as confused as Blake felt.

She just shook her head. "I have no idea." Nothing about this made sense. She would do some digging when she got home. But the further away they drove from the house, the more the thoughts and memories of the woman seemed to fade too, as if it had all been a dream.

That night, Blake and Ella made dinner together. It was the first time they'd done that since before Warren had passed. Blake also got a phone call from the police. The red notebook contained the banking information to the off-shore account the sisters had been sending the embezzled money to. They were also able to confirm that it was the sisters who had acquired all the gambling debt, not Warren. So Blake would no longer be responsible for any of it.

For the first time in a long time, Blake felt relief from the pressure that had been pushing her under for the past year. Someone knocked on the door. She opened it to find Jack standing there, looking terribly nervous.

"Hi," he said, shifting from foot to foot. "Is Ella home?"

Before Blake could respond, Ella came up beside her.

"Hey," she said, smiling.

His cheeks pinked a little and he smiled. "Hey."

They stared at each other for a moment before Jack seemed to remember why he had come. "Oh, I uh, came to return your shoe." He held it up.

"Oh my gosh! Thank you!"

Jack shrugged. "Glad I could help. They're pretty unique shoes. Where did you get them?"

There was an awkward silence as Ella glanced at Blake. She racked her mind, unable to remember. She made a face and shrugged.

Ella turned back to Jack. "There's a little frozen yogurt shop a few blocks from here. Would you like to get some with me?"

He smiled. "I would love that."

"Perfect. I'll just grab my *other* shoes." She gave Blake a quick kiss on the cheek. "Be back soon."

Healing spread back through the parts of Blake that had believed she'd lost Ella forever. As she closed the door, Blake's phone dinged.

Instantly, a smile split her face.

Cam: Hey, how are you feeling?

Blake: Better than you, probably.

Cam: I doubt it. This really beautiful woman kissed me yesterday. I'm still not sure I didn't just dream it all up.

Blake's heart beat madly. She bit her lip, still grinning like an idiot.

Cam: I might have to try it again, just to make sure it was real. If she'll let me.

A soft knock made Blake's stomach flip. Slowly, almost timidly, she turned the handle and pulled open her door just enough to peer out. Cam stood there, one hand in his pocket, the other holding his phone. A bruise had come in over his cheekbone.

"How do I know you're not a serial killer?" she asked.

He shrugged, grinning wickedly. "You don't."

She smiled but still, she didn't move. Despite everything that had happened, despite how much she wanted this, there was still a fear that squirmed through her thoughts that eventually, he would decide he didn't want her after all. That he would leave, just like everyone else.

It was like Cam could hear her thoughts because he stepped closer. "Don't be afraid of me," he said, his eyes worried.

"I'm trying," she whispered. Slowly, she opened the door and he stepped inside just enough to let the door close behind them. He turned, setting his hands against the wall on either side of her face, holding her in place but also giving her space to leave if she chose.

Her body instantly reacted to his nearness, flushing hot. But beneath that, something awakened, something she'd thought she'd lost long ago as a small child when her parent's indifference taught her she wasn't important, something she'd thought had died when her first love left her for her best friend. Hope. Hope that someone could love her. Hope that someone would choose her.

"I have something I need to ask you," he said, and Blake was surprised to find a hint of fear there.

"Okay," she said.

He searched her eyes, slowly drawing in a long, deep breath.

"Will *you* stay? You already own my heart, but if you don't want it, I need to know here and now. I'm asking you to be honest with me, Blake. I... I *need* you to be honest with me."

Blake thought about what he had told her about his fiance. Until this moment, it hadn't occurred to her that perhaps he felt as unwanted as she did, that this was just as terrifying for him as it was for her.

"So," he said. "I'm asking you to stay. Stay. With. Me," he whispered.

Blake reached for his face, his stubble gently scratching the palms of her hands. Slowly, she pulled his head down until his lips touched hers. Instantly, his fingers dug into her hair, his mouth devouring hers, pulling, tasting, exploring. He breathed her name, making her heart split and shatter and start to heal all at once. She let him taste her hunger for him, giving him all the vulnerability she had. He took it in, accepting it all.

Blake pulled back, touching her forehead to his.

"I'll stay."

THE END

About the Author

Serene Heiner is the creative soul behind the growing Instagram and TikTok accounts @magicalbooknook. When she's not writing, drawing, sewing, taking book photos, making videos, or crafting, (deep breath) she can be found either participating in her workout group or training for her next Spartan race. Serene is a diehard fantasy reader but can be caught cheating on the genre from time to time. She's a proud mother to seven little readers and lives with them and her husband in their home in Idaho where books are stacked to the ceiling. Where does she find the time to write? The world may never know.

www.ingramcontent.com/pod-product-compliance
Lightning Source LLC
Chambersburg PA
CBHW070648130626
46555CB00006B/2775